# FIREFLY

*Columbus Day*
*Another Elvis Love Child*
*Angel of Brooklyn*
*Little Bones*

# Firefly

## Janette Jenkins

Chatto & Windus

LONDON

Published by Chatto & Windus 2013

2 4 6 8 10 9 7 5 3 1

First published in Great Britain in 2013 by
Chatto & Windus
Random House, 20 Vauxhall Bridge Road,
London SW1V 2SA

www.randomhouse.co.uk

Addresses for companies within The Random House Group Limited can be
found at: www.randomhouse.co.uk/offices.htm

The Random House Group Limited Reg. No. 954009

A CIP catalogue record for this book
is available from the British Library

ISBN 9780701187422

The Random House Group Limited supports the Forest Stewardship
Council® (FSC®), the leading international forest-certification organisation.
Our books carrying the FSC label are printed on FSC®-certified paper.
FSC is the only forest-certification scheme supported by the leading
environmental organisations, including Greenpeace. Our paper
procurement policy can be found at
www.randomhouse.co.uk/environment

Typeset in Janson by Palimpsest Book Production Limited,
Falkirk, Stirlingshire

Printed and bound by
CPI Group (UK) Ltd, Croydon CR0 4YY

For Dad
With Love
1940–2002

'I *am* England; and England is me.'

Noël Coward, *Sunday Express*, 1965

'If you're a star, you should behave like one.
I always have.'

Noël Coward, *Sunday Times*, 1969

# ONE

# I

## Firefly, Port Maria, Jamaica
## 1971

THE SKY is a wavering sheet of blue and when the lilo stays in one place it feels like he's flying, suspended halfway between heaven and no-man's-land. He pushes his sunglasses from his forehead down to his eyes. The lenses are dark but pinkish: he would not like Jamaica to be grey. The swimming pool makes a constant splashing as his fingertips trail across the pale bouncy water. He pictures his breakfast: the plate of fruit, the toast already cold, the glass of mango juice. He feels hungry, but he can't quite face the undignified scrambling. At seventy-one he can no longer leap and soar from the deep end to the pool edge. Now, it's a fumbling heave-ho at the steps with the water dragging him down.

Firefly: the retreat he built from Captain Morgan's Lookout. A place so small no visitor can stay overnight. Down the hill, his other house, his 'real' Jamaican house, will be bustling with breakfast trays, screeching voices and sly aperitifs. Pool towels will be drying on the rocks, their tails flapping. Opinions will be aired and repeated. Gossip.

Closing his eyes, feeling the tilt and motion of the airbed, he makes lists. Occupations. English counties. Girls' names beginning with A, B, and so on. At Vanessa the lure of breakfast becomes too strong and he navigates himself to the steps, slipping and sweating, with so much water falling from his body he wonders where it has been hiding.

Sitting on a towel he eats methodically. With his eyes closed he would not be able to distinguish the papaya from the melon. The toast is dry. His glass of mango juice is a thick pulpy sugar.

On the terrace a servant sweeps dust from underneath the chairs. He moves slowly, a cigarette hanging between his large white teeth.

'Where's Miguel?' asks Noël.

'Week off, Boss. Hot day.'

'I'm not complaining, Patrice,' he says, squinting at the sky.

4

'I went down to Blue Harbour to collect up the mail, I fetched a nice piece of fish for your lunch.'

'I don't want fish, I can't be bothered with it.'

As Patrice flicks the broom, Noël can see the sweat glistening on his forehead. A dark strip of skin where his shirt rides over his belt-line.

'Could you get me a drink?'

The broom stops. 'Tea, Boss?'

'Coca-Cola.'

'Coming right up, Boss. A Coke.'

With the sun burning his cheekbones he moves into the shade. His mail sits on a table. He looks at the handwriting. Small. Neat. Veering sharply to the left. He examines the stamps: two English and a Canadian.

His drink arrives clanging with ice cubes; a jagged slice of lime.

'Will you be taking your walk before or after lunch?' asks Patrice.

Noël groans. He blinks at the sunlight and lights another cigarette. 'Isn't it too hot?'

'Mr Payn said we should walk the back way, where it's always cool, and always full of the shade.'

'Good old Mr Payn.'

'The walk is for your health, Boss.'

'I can't believe it's come to this. Walking.'

'We could stop at Ronnie's Bar.'

'You're on.' Though Noël wonders how far it is to Ronnie's. Has he been there before? Is it safe?

He opens the first of his letters. It's from the actress Judy Campbell and her news and heartfelt wishes make him smile. The other two are from strangers asking for his picture.

Fizzing with Coca-Cola he goes inside to dress. The rooms are full of shadows. A small yellow butterfly clings to the wardrobe where his Hawaiian-style shirts hang shoulder to shoulder, smelling of soap and insect repellent. He chooses a pink number. Beige slacks. He wishes Miguel was here. Miguel would have helped him with the fasteners, the slippery buckle, the small fiddly buttons that don't seem to fit inside the buttonholes. By the time he's managed all fifteen, he doesn't know whether to shout, 'Hurrah!' or to burst into tears.

Exhausted, he sits on the end of the bed and lights another cigarette. Through the glowing window he can see Patrice with a net in his hand leaning over the pool. The sunlight is dazzling. When he closes his eyes a red silhouette stays with him in the darkness.

'Boss? Are you awake? We should walk, Boss.' Patrice is standing in the doorway. The hems of his trousers are wet; his feet are dripping with water.

'Walk?'

6

'Yes, Boss, before it gets too hot.'

'It's already too hot,' says Noël.

'You promised Mr Payn, remember?'

'Is Graham coming up today?' he asks.

'He didn't say, Boss, but he did say, I should make you do your walking.'

Noël examines his feet bulging from his espadrilles. The ropey soles are tattered. He won't get far in these.

'Could you look for my sandals?' he asks.

Leaving a trail of wet footprints Patrice pads around the rooms, until eventually he finds them under the bed, wedged between *The Songs of Kander & Ebb* and a tin of milk wafers.

'I wonder?' says Noël, suddenly embarrassed. 'Could you possibly?' And as Patrice bends to slip the sandals onto his boss's swollen feet, to tighten the straps, Noël pictures the shoe shops in England, the scent of the leather, the metal device that measures the length and breadth of your feet.

'I'm feeling particularly nostalgic today,' he says, taking Patrice by the elbow. 'I've been thinking about home.'

'Switzerland?'

'London.'

'That suits me fine, Boss,' he says.

Outside, the heat assaults his senses. He reaches

for his sunglasses. 'I didn't need a pair of these in London. Not really. Though I wore them to protect my eyes from the smog, or if I was feeling very Hollywood.'

Patrice laughs. 'Now, I can't stand wearing glasses of any kind, Boss. They make my face all tense, like my head is a wall with something clinging onto it. I usually get a headache.'

Their progress is slow. Noël stops and starts, occasionally affecting an interest in a plant, a low-swooping bird, or the anaemic long-tailed lizards. He can feel his shirt sticking to the small of his back, as the sea appears below them, like something he could easily fall into, a deep shiny bath where he'd be weightless; floating.

'I've seen the sun shining in London, Mr Coward,' says Patrice, as they lean against a tree trunk, lighting cigarettes.

'You've been to London?'

'Not yet, Boss, but I've seen the picture postcards and the sky looked very blue.'

'They paint it,' Noël tells him. 'There are factories where the painters dip their brushes into the brightest blue they can find. They cover up the grey in all the photographs. Sometimes, if you look very hard, you can still see their brushstrokes.'

'Is that true, Mr Coward?'

'Perfectly true,' he says.

'I don't believe it.'

'But think about it. Who would want to buy a postcard full of filthy rainclouds?'

'My God!' Patrice laughs, slapping his hands across his knees. 'You are right!'

They traipse a little further. Noël can feel an aching in his ankles. The ground is loose and he has to work hard to get a grip on it. 'I think we've come far enough,' he pants. 'My circulation is grateful and the blood is pumping nicely through my veins.'

'I thought we were going to Ronnie's?'

'Were we? Is it far?'

'Another ten minutes, Boss. Twenty at this pace.'

'I think we should turn around before you have to carry me back. We'll have a drink at the house. We can dangle our feet in the swimming pool.'

Noël can feel the impatience in Patrice's right arm as he stops, starts, and lumbers. He loves the heat, but today his chest feels like it might be rattling with explosives. Flaming. He almost wishes for rain.

His pool appears like a mirage. Noël sits at the edge and pulls off his sandals. When he lets his feet fall into the water, he's surprised there isn't steam.

'Drink, Boss?'

'I'll have a vodka tonic and get one for yourself.'

'A beer, Boss?'

'Anything.'

They sit side by side, Patrice sipping his beer delicately, licking the pale popping foam from his lips.

'It's not a bad life,' says Noël.

Patrice exhales loudly. 'Not a bad life, Boss, but I do keep thinking . . .'

'Thinking what?'

'That I would like to be a waiter, Boss.'

Noël's mouth twitches; he tries to swallow a smile. 'Well, I do like a man with ambition.'

'Not just any waitering, Boss. Silver service, the best. Would you like to eat lunch now? I could practise it.'

Noël shakes his head. His stomach feels tight. His guts are fizzing with gas. 'No lunch and no silver service. Too much clattering.'

Swinging his legs from the pool, Patrice stands and shakes the water from his feet. Noël can feel the droplets on his elbow: a scattering of bee stings.

Inside the house Patrice swerves around the dining chairs, nodding, bowing, holding wide imaginary platters which he lowers to the table with a flourish.

'I can see you, Patrice, and you'd be sacked like a shot from any play of mine.'

'I would, Boss? Why?'

'Too much business and you're overacting to buggery. Waiters should be discreet and invisible.'

'I'll add that to my list, Mr Coward,' he says, with his head through the window. 'Rule number two. Discreet and invisible.'

'And rule number one?'

'Always check the zipper on your flies.'

Wincing, Noël looks at his feet floating in the water. They make him think of lard. He closes his eyes. He hears the click-clack of the insects. The ripples as they lick against the concrete.

*'Patrice!'*

Patrice moves slowly, wiping his hands on his cream-coloured trousers. He stops.

'Did you not hear me shouting?' says Noël.

'Sorry, Boss. I had the radio on.'

'The Light Programme?'

'Bob Marley! Reggae! Reggae!'

'How very native of you. And what's with all this waiter business anyway? Don't you like working for me?'

'Oh yes, Boss,' he says, brushing an insect from his hair. 'Very much. And I like Mr Payn and Mr Cole. Such comedians.'

'You think so?' Noël pulls off his glasses, leaving a dent across the soft doughy bridge of his nose.

11

'Oh, most definitely, Boss. But I am hoping to go to the Ritz.'

'So, they're opening a branch down in Kingston? How very forward-thinking.'

'The hotel is in London, Boss. I am wanting to go to London, England.'

'You'll freeze your balls off in London.'

Wriggling backwards, Noël manages to release his legs from the water, though they refuse to co-operate when he thinks about standing. It seems such a long way up.

'Help me.'

Patrice holds out his hands, and after much heaving and panting, Noël makes it into the chair. He feels cumbersome. Awkward. He would like to disappear.

At the side of the pool Patrice hovers, chewing his bottom lip. He traces a wobbly question mark with the dusty tip of his shoe. 'I was wondering, Boss,' he starts. 'I was wondering about a letter. You know. A reference. My cousin is going to England next week. He'll be staying in a place called Brixton.'

'Courtesy of Her Majesty? How very bijou.'

'Oh no, Boss, he's sailing with Fyffe's. He has a friend who works at the Ritz, he knows the manager very well, and the manager is expecting a hand-delivered letter from Sir Noël Coward, regarding his servant, Patrice.'

Noël runs his tongue across his damp top lip. 'I don't think you'd be happy there. The Ritz is very white, front of house.'

'But I'd be happy doing kitchen work, I can wash dishes, I can peel a potato in ten seconds flat.'

'Well, I can see you're highly qualified, though why you'd want to work in a kitchen, never seeing the light of day, is beyond me.'

'My dream is in the waitering.'

'Then I'll keep my fingers crossed.'

'And the reference, Mr Coward?'

'Will be thundering with applause.'

'Thank you. So you'll write the letter soon? I have to take it to Joe.'

'Joe?'

'My cousin, Joe.'

'Would Mr Payn not do it?'

'Mr Payn is not like you, Boss. He is not well known at the Ritz.'

'I think you will find that in some areas of that splendid hotel, he is intimately known.'

'The manager, Boss.'

'Will deny it.'

Noël turns. He pulls a fleck of loose tobacco from his teeth. 'To tell you the truth, I'm not over fond of the Ritz,' he says. 'The place is full of tourists lingering over tea.'

'But it is the best hotel in the world, Mr Coward! I have seen pictures of the rooms, I have heard from other people, it has the best chefs, the best waiters, extremely smart uniforms—'

'Will you shut the fuck up about the blessed Ritz hotel?'

'I'm only saying, Boss.'

'Don't.'


Siesta. Beneath his flickering eyelids his long-dead father opens long brown envelopes. Bills. His mother, fingering her pearls, is throwing a strained, *but let's look on the bright side* expression. The mantel clock ticks. Snow falls across the windowpane, blocking out the light.

Noël can't see himself, but he knows he's wearing blue pyjamas and soft red slippers. He's been ill. Coughing. It might be something tubercular. A few stray snowflakes fall sizzling into the fireplace. Above his head the floorboards are creaking: his younger brother Eric is pacing up and down.

The lodgers appear. Unassuming and polite. Noël hopes they can't see his pyjamas, a cheap pair from Brown's on the high street. The lodgers seem embarrassed to be here, to be taking up the chairs in the Cowards' dining room, but Noël can see that his mother looks happier already, her cheeks are rosy, and she's laughing, serving bowls of brown Windsor soup, pouring water, ignoring her husband who has to help himself.

Noël appears to be floating. He looks down on the table from somewhere near the light sconce on the ceiling. He can see the steam rising from the soup bowls, plates of white rolls, yellow curls of butter. The lodger with the narrow hunched shoulders scratches the back of his neck. 'Snow,' he's saying; 'it will fill up the hospitals. Always does. Bones will be snapping like breadsticks.' Noël can see his father grinning, his mouth over-wide, like he's trying too hard to be affable.

And then he's outside, looking at the house with its row of yellow windows. The railings are filling with snow. Women walk past, battling the weather, coat hems dragging, umbrellas pressed in front of their lowered faces, flimsy shields of black, green, indigo, they push against the swirling flakes and a wind blows up, though Noël feels nothing but buoyant, sailing towards Miss Thomas's Dancing Academy on the other side of town.

Usually, Noël makes his way there on the bus. He'll entertain himself by talking to strangers. The woman with the hairpiece. The man trying to concentrate on

15

his newspaper: the obituaries. A girl in pain with a toothache. Sometimes, Noël will hone his acting skills by sobbing, and tears flowing, he'll tell a wretched story, about his fare being stolen, or his mother on death's door. His hand will be patted. Or his knee. A sixpence found. And once he was taken to a teashop for buns and lemonade, because, as the clerical gentleman said, 'You do need cheering up.'

Hovering at the frozen sash window he can see rows of dimpled, chubby-kneed girls holding out the hems of their pale pink skirts, doing clumsy steps and twirls. Their faces are full of bemused concentration, the mirror reflecting the snow, now coming down in curtains, a stern Miss Thomas tapping her bamboo cane in time to the shuddering music.

Noël moves on. It feels like he's swimming. Over spiny bare trees. The buses waiting in line. Harrods glitters. A few stray men, their dark woollen overcoats now brushed with white, scuttle into Fortnum & Mason. Piccadilly Circus has vanished, London is all mixed up – Liberty's sits next to Westminster Bridge, the Thames appears to be flowing down the Mall; a fine lace shroud covers everything.

Opening his eyes, Noël can see the snow, though it seems to have slackened and when the sun comes through, it isn't snow at all but the little heads of jasmine.

'We're taking the car if you need anything.' Noël can hear Graham's voice through the window. 'Has he asked for anything special?'

'No, Mr Payn.'

'Did he eat the fish?'

'He didn't fancy the fish, Boss.'

'What did he eat?'

'A cheese sandwich.'

'And the walk?'

'Oh, we walked all right,' says Patrice, with a chuckle in his voice. 'I made him do the walking.'

'Very good, well done.'

'Will you and Mr Cole be coming up tonight?'

'No, we're going to a party and he doesn't want to join us. He's afraid they'll make him sing for his supper, they usually do, you know.'

Noël can hear their shoes scraping. A clearing of the throat. He hears Graham laughing. The revving of the car's fitful engine.

He sits in his dressing gown watching a large black fly skating over the wall. He counts to thirty-nine before it reaches the side of the mirror frame. If he stares at his paintings without blinking, the crowds start scuttling, the fish tails flap inside the baskets, and all the handsome boys start taking off their clothes.

Feet up. The shadows splayed across the ceiling

are wet crumpled roses. He wriggles his toes. A plume of cigarette smoke hovers like a damp sheet of mist. He eats three buttered cream crackers. An orange.

He sifts through his LP records. Judy Garland. Tommy Steele. Johnnie Ray will do. The Nabob of Sob. 'Cry'. Noël tugs at his sleeves. He looks through the window. The garden is empty. The record is miserable. What did he expect? He clicks it off and picks out 'The Trolley Song'. Too clangy.

He finds a new pad of paper and draws circles across the first three lines. He thinks of names and occupations. Jake Fellowes: Photographer. Jill Reid: Devoted Wife and Mother. Sam Heron: Petty Officer. He can see them. The way they move. Laugh. They don't have a story, but at least they've been christened. He writes Act One, Scene One: A Small Country Hotel.

Underneath a cushion he finds a red button. He has no idea where it came from. In the cabinet an old toffee tin holds stray buttons, tie clips, and other odds and ends. He prises off the lid and drops the button into it. Then he tips the contents onto the table. He makes patterns. It absorbs him. A bottle cap becomes a slightly bashed sun. The tie clips look like trees.

'Should I run you a bath, Mr Coward?'
    'Where's Miguel?'

'Week off, Boss.'

'Is it time for my bath?'

'Almost six-thirty.'

'Then run me a bath,' he says.

Lying across the bed he can hear the gushing water. He glances at the old children's book on the dresser. *The Wouldbegoods* by E. Nesbit. As a child he took it from the library and renewed it every week. He was Miss Nesbit's biggest fan. *The Enchanted Castle* was his favourite, *Five Children and It* coming close second with seventeen back-to-back renewals, much to the chagrin of the owlish librarian who could see no rule to say the boy couldn't do it. The book is foxed. On page 19 a teacup stain circles the chapter heading.

Patrice is whistling and it sets his teeth on edge. It isn't a tuneless whistle, but it's grating all the same. Out of memory a song floods his brain and overrides the background din. It's one of his favourites, Bernard Cribbins, 'Hole, in the Ground'. He starts singing. *'There was I, digging this hole, hole in the ground, so big and sort of round . . .'*

The bath water swallows him. The bubbles cover his stomach and put him in mind of a pudding. He slides down. The bathroom here is basic. Tiny. He thinks of the black and white tiles of the Jazz Age. Steam rooms. The mirrored shelves of Dior, Chanel,

Penhaligon's. Sometimes he'd pull in a chair, and he'd lie in the bath chatting merrily away to whoever might be about. Gert perhaps. Gertrude Lawrence could talk the hind legs off a donkey, usually moaning about her script, her part, or her love life. Marlene was the same. If it wasn't Yul Brynner (*Oh, but I adore the cruel Russian bastard*) it was the bitter Kraut press. If a man was there it might turn into something else. He imagines the warm wet mouth of that young taxi driver. Dave? Gerry? Bob? He was blond, he had soft, light bristles; a sharply upturned nose.

When he opens his eyes he thinks he might have nodded off. Through the window the small strip of sky has turned violet. The water feels cold. He can see his monogrammed towel on the rail, the rubber mat to stop him slipping. Patrice has disappeared, leaping down the hill. He said he'd be back in twenty minutes. Noël can see his wristwatch on the table, he can hear it ticking, but he can't reach it – he can't read the time.

And then the room appears to be swinging, the walls coming remarkably close to his face, the heat making him dizzy, the sudden sharp lurch into a vertical position. Pausing, taking his life into his hands, he perches on the shiny lip of the bath tub and attempts to get his breath back. The water runs from his shoulder blades using the dip of his spine as

20

a race track. The bubbles have long gone. His feet are standing in an ever-widening puddle.

'Patrice!'

He pulls himself towards the towels and dabs his chest dry. The talc shower makes him cough. Leaving milky footprints he holds the wall gingerly with the tips of his fingers and makes it into the bedroom, where Patrice has left his clothes out. More fucking buttons.

'Did you need me, Boss?'

For a minute Noël can't speak. He's discarded the belt. He's had it with belts. 'Where did you bugger off to? I could have bashed my brains out on the floor tiles.'

'Sorry, Boss. Emergency.'

'Life or death?'

'Cigarettes.'

Sitting on the end of the bed, Noël rubs a handkerchief over his face. A gecko skitters across the door frame. He can feel his jaw tightening.

'I need a drink,' he says. 'What time will Graham be here with the cocktails?'

'He won't be here, Boss. He's going to a party.'

'What party? Whose?'

Patrice shrugs. 'I didn't ask, Boss.'

'Why the fuck not, you useless piece of shit? Hell. Will Mr Cole be going with him?'

'I think that's what he said.'

'You think?' Noël bangs his fists into the mattress. 'What about me?' he whines, pummelling his hands. 'Who the fuck am I going to talk to? What about my cocktail? Bastards.'

'Should I call them, Boss?'

'Yes. No. *Fuck it.*'

Later. Noël sips his Martell and ginger looking at the garden. He watches the swifts dipping into his swimming pool. Above his head the stars are fat and glittering, their sharp light catching the roll of the sea like lighthouse beams; they flicker over the ships, they target the small bobbing fishing boats, yachts. He pictures the men at the dockside wearing faded T-shirts, smoking joints and cheap cigarettes.

He can see his brother sitting in the opposite chair. He has his ankles crossed. He's wearing tennis whites. His face looks stony. Sullen. Perhaps Eric has fallen out with their mother again? Or Aunt Vida? Or is it another one of those episodes when he resents his brother's success? *Oh, it's all right for some, having a fleet of fancy new cars! And now you've sent me to Ceylon and I'm broken.*

Patrice breaks the spell. 'I fried some sausages, Boss,' he says. 'And I heated up the cold mashed potato and the peas.'

'Where's everyone else?'

'Out, Boss. Somewhere.'

'Do we have ketchup?' asks Noël, rubbing his eyes and getting slowly to his feet.

'Yes, Boss.'

'Really? We do? Is it Heinz?'

## 2

ACROSS THE beach bodies are strewn like flotsam and jetsam. There are red parasols, abandoned flip-flops, snorkels. Two men with wheat-coloured hair play a lazy bat and ball. Standing in the waves, a man in a tight Pepsi T-shirt holds a long loose fishing line. Between two rocks a large transistor radio plays Jimmy Cliff's, 'Wonderful World, Beautiful People'.

Noël sits to one side beneath a wide umbrella. His nose, raw from yesterday's sun, is plastered with a thick white lotion. He's wearing shorts and a loose Hawaiian shirt. His nude bathing days are over, he can't imagine his body ever reverting into the shape of the rippled tanned specimens he's looking at, however hard he tries, however much he lays off the sugar, the butter, the full-cream milk.

Graham is lying on his front with his feet in the

24

water, reading an old *Reader's Digest* magazine. At fifty-three he's still trim, his dark hair showing a few signs of grey. He's wearing nothing but a tiny pair of black and white trunks, his skin is freshly oiled and glistening like caramel.

'Look at him,' Noël says to Coley, who's appeared at his side with a plate of black grapes. '*Reader's Digest*? He always was an illiterate little sod.' He takes the grapes, holding the bunch aloft, pulling a few loose with his teeth, like some spoilt ancient emperor.

Coley is a sharp wiry man, buzzing with nervous energy. 'Is the music too much?' he asks.

'No,' says Noël. 'In fact, I rather like it.'

'Is it too busy?'

Noël shakes his head. 'As long as they keep their distance,' he says, circling his hand into the royal wave as one of the bathers salutes him.

When he closes his eyes, the noise seems far away, the lapping waves, the chattering throb of the radio; a breeze pats at the umbrella.

'Have you had a walk around?' a voice asks. He opens his eyes. A face appears to be hovering above him. It takes a good few seconds for the face to turn into Graham.

'I walked from the car,' he says. 'Is that not far enough?'

'How about to the sea and back?'

Noël can feel himself prickling. The sand is too soft. There are stones and bony seashells. 'Do I have to? Now?'

Graham shrugs. 'I can't make you,' he says, walking away.

Noël swallows. The sun presses against his shins. Blistering. He lights another cigarette as someone laughs hysterically. The hot air reeks of baked sand, perfumed oil, sweat.

They eat shrimp for lunch and though Noël wants to stamp his feet, to say, *Not for me, too fiddly*, he takes the plate he's offered, shuffling forward so it can rest easier on his knees, and he proceeds to pull and tear at the shellfish, a worthless task when all he manages to pop into his mouth is the smallest piece of tail. He looks around. Everyone else is lounging in the sand, picking with their fingers. Did no one think to bring the foldaway table? When the table was here they'd have a linen cloth, crockery and decanters.

'Coley!' he shouts.

'Yes?' Coley appears in less than twenty seconds, licking mayonnaise from his fingers.

'Where's Miguel?' asks Noël, shading his eyes and squinting into the distance.

'He's with his family. You told him to stay with his cousin for the week. He'll be back with us on Monday. Did you want something?'

Noël looks at the mess on his plate. 'Some fucking edible food would be nice.'

'Chicken? Cold ham? A sandwich?'

'Oh, just get me a drink,' he says.

The wine tastes sharp and it makes his eyes water. A man walks the length of the beach on his hands. This watching is exhausting. When someone waves or calls out a greeting Noël has no idea of their name. Some of them look familiar. The boy with the inflatable palm tree. The one with the anchor tattoo.

'Yoo-hoo!' shouts the man with the fishing line, his damp T-shirt riding high over his flat solar plexus. 'I think I've frightened the blighters, I've hooked nothing all morning.'

'Don't I count?' says the boy with the palm tree (deflated).

'Apart from Ted. I did hook Ted.'

'Good-oh,' says Noël, circling his cigarette somewhere to the side of him. 'Now, could you please recommend the bait?'

They laugh and shake their heads. Noël's heart is tripping. The people look like insects who are just about to swarm. He thinks of the swimming pool at Firefly. The empty garden. Bed.

'Coley!' he bellows. 'Could someone take me up the hill? I've had enough! For fuck's sake! *Coley!*'

\* \* \*

27

As the car shifts gear, the sun almost melting the glass, Noël can see Patrice standing at the top of the steps, his hands on his hips, unmoving.

'Well, he's working hard,' the driver chuckles. 'I'll bet he hasn't stopped for a minute all morning.'

Noël says nothing. His bare legs are sticking to the cracked vinyl seat. Between his feet a canvas bag is bursting with packets of English biscuits, loose tea, apples.

Stepping out of the car he loses his left espadrille. The driver picks it up, slamming it onto the wing, before Noël attempts to squeeze it back onto his rather pink foot. Patrice takes the bag, letting it swing from his fingers as if it weighs nothing.

'Will you be needing the car again, Massa?' The driver pulls a chequered handkerchief from his pocket and passes it over his forehead.

'Not today, thank you.'

Watching Patrice strutting into the house Noël makes his way slowly up the path. He concentrates on the ground, avoiding the potholes and the broken stone flags. A few pink flowers are bursting from the bushes. They remind him of bubblegum. When he reaches the steps Patrice reappears, holding out his hand.

'Your face is very red, Boss,' he says. 'And your nose is very white.'

*   *   *

28

A restless siesta. His eyelids are prickling. He tries counting sheep. Heartbeats. He pictures other rooms he has slept in. Guest rooms. Austere barracks. Hotel suites. Hospitals. He thinks of the bedrooms of his childhood. The pale blue stripes of the box room. Thick flannel pyjamas. Pressed against his cheek, his hands would smell of sweetened milk; of Pears transparent soap.

Sometimes, after his mother had kissed him goodnight, he would kneel on the bed, pushing his head between the curtains, before sweeping them wide with a flourish. The view was nothing more than other houses and other squares of light but he would imagine the lives inside. The ironing of party frocks. A nanny darning stockings. The rippling ivory keys of a piano, perhaps sold to them by his father, Mr Arthur Sabin Coward, who it has to be said spent more time bemoaning his lot and cursing the weather than doing much in the way of selling anything that might earn him more than a stipend of commission.

With his nose against the glass Noël imagined the faces looking back at him. *Who is that remarkable-looking boy at the back of our neighbour's house?* If only their sons had an ounce of his charm they'd be laughing. And as he pulled the curtains (*slowly now, slowly, wait for it . . .*) he would give them a flick of a bow before closing the last few inches, slipping into the grey fuzzy darkness of his bedroom, where undoubtedly he would dream of the blinding footlights. His name on a playbill. The curtain going up.

In Jamaica he opens his eyes and stares at the ceiling fan; the black cord dangling. Should he take a sleeping pill? Half a sleeping pill? The bottle sits by his lamp like a squat sergeant major. He rattles it. His water glass is empty.

Eventually, he drifts off for twenty minutes. He doesn't dream of his childhood, his on-off sleep is nothing but a thin dismal curtain with the light passing through it.

When the car pulls up he's climbing *The Tower of Mystery* with the six Bastable children. He closes the book. Squints. The car is empty, apart from the driver who seems to be examining a tooth in the rear-view mirror.

'I said I didn't need you,' Noël tells him.

'Yes, Massa,' says the driver, jiggling the keys. 'Mr Payn sent me, Massa. He said I was to take you to the barber's.'

Noël can feel himself sinking. 'That was today?'

'Yes, Massa.'

'Oh hell and fucking damnation.'

'Yes, Massa.'

He sits in the front with the driver, Patrice sprawled

30

across the back seat as they bounce from pothole to pothole, passing mule carts, battered public buses, a woman plaiting a small girl's hair. The sky is clouding over. The air feels sticky. Solid. The driver puts his hand towards the radio, before pulling it back again.

In Port Maria they stop in what might just pass as a car park, the cars parked at all angles, people selling plastic washing bowls, batteries, eggs. The air has a dense fishy smell. A woman selling grapefruit is being assaulted on all sides by a buzzing cape of flies.

'I'll wait here, Massa,' says the driver, already adjusting his seat into a more relaxed, supine position. 'You take your time now, Massa. Okay?'

They move stumbling towards the barber's shop, Patrice kicking stones and whistling through his teeth. Music pours from open shutters and doors. The air on every corner is pulsing with Bob Marley, Millie, and ska. Through a shop window Noël can see a woman dancing, and with a gelatinous roll of her hips she weaves joyously between the groaning shelves of guava jelly, coconut water and the giant drums of cooking fat.

The barber, Mr Dennis, is sitting with his feet on a stool reading a copy of the *Gleaner*, though as soon as he sees Noël, he springs to attention, throws down the paper and wipes his inky hands on his short white coat, adding to the smears along the hemline. He offers a hand to Noël. 'Here we are again, Sir Noël, Mr Coward. Why, it don't seem like five minutes ago I was standing here trimming the back of your neck.'

'I've tried talking to what little hair I have left, but it won't listen, whatever I say, and however hard I wag my finger, it will insist on growing.'

Mr Dennis laughs, turning the old leather chair to face his customer, and as Noël sinks into it gratefully, a boy jumps to pull the cord of the ceiling fan. The boy, about eight years old, is wearing dirty white plimsolls and an overlong shirt with frills on the chest, giving him the air of a small tawdry choirboy.

'Can I get you a drink?' asks Mr Dennis. 'A beer? A malt? A glass of fruit and ginger?'

'No, thank you,' says Noël. 'Should we just get on with it?'

Through the large oval mirror he lets his eyes drift. He looks at the things on the counter, the waxes, the ashtray, the pointed plastic combs in varying shades of yellow. Across the walls pictures pulled from magazines have been taped in short haphazard lines. Men with ploughed glossy waves, dense black haloes, beads.

The boy shakes out a towel and wraps it around Noël's neck, while Mr Dennis sharpens his scissors. In the background Patrice sits with his arms folded, before succumbing to the pile of dog-eared magazines.

'The usual, Sir Noël?'

'The usual,' he says, and Mr Dennis starts removing the excess, the hair that's almost sitting inside his collar, the curling grey ends scattering like question marks.

Mr Dennis hums. 'Looks like there's rain on the way,' he says. 'I can feel it sitting in the heat. Heavy. Have you been busy, Sir Noël? Have you been writing any plays?'

Noël grunts. Patrice looks up from his magazine and grins. The fan above their heads starts stuttering and the boy has to jerk the cord, grunting as his fingers grope to reach the swaying end of it. Noël feels tense. When he lifts his eyes to his reflection it seems he is looking at an overgrown reptile. He feels the familiar lurch of disappointment. He looks away. Whatever happened to the facelift?

'Fast enough for you, Sir Noël?' Mr Dennis, smiling wryly, is brushing the back of his neck.

'Perfect.' Noël fishes in his pockets for change, then realising there's nothing inside but the creased cotton lining, he looks helplessly towards Patrice, who opens his wallet and pays.

The driver has fallen asleep, his head across the steering wheel, his mouth gaping open like an over-fed guppy fish. The air is suffocating. A girl in a flowery dress chases a small skinny cockerel with a stick. When

Noël removes his sunglasses the people in the car park look like they are melting.

'You all right, Boss?'

'Hot.'

'We could go to the Lagoon. Jimmy will let you have a tab.'

'Will it be quiet?' asks Noël.

'As a rock.'

'Perfect.'

Noël steps into the bar with some apprehension. The only other customers are five local men, sitting around a table playing a serious game of cards. The men, wrinkled like forgotten windfall apples, hardly raise their eyes as Noël finds an empty booth and presses himself into it. Through the open window the sea looks dull. Metallic. It reminds him of Dover. He can hear Patrice laughing at the bar. The card players are muttering as they throw down queens and aces.

Jimmy the owner appears with Patrice and the drinks. Noël tries his best to look agreeable.

'How good it is to see you, Sir Noël,' says Jimmy, a tall bony man with a garish sense of dress (purple and yellow today). 'I always say it is a great pleasure and an honour to serve such a dignified gentleman, and one who brings all sorts of people to the island, from the Queen to Liz Taylor.'

'I'm glad you approve,' says Noël, his fingers fumbling for a fresh cigarette.

'Approve? Who could not approve of Liz Taylor? She is gorgeousness personified. A goddess.'

'I couldn't agree more.'

'I don't suppose you have her number?' says Jimmy, leaning closer. 'I do get lonely on the weekends.'

Patrice laughs. 'And what will you say to Pearl? Oh, I'm sorry, Pearl, I can't take you dancin', I got me a smokin' hot date with Miss Taylor . . .'

'True.' Jimmy frowns. 'Pearl would kill me. She would cut off my testicles and feed them to the dogs. Still, it might just be worth it.'

'I think you should know, Miss Taylor has expensive taste,' says Noël. 'She's excessively fond of very large diamonds.'

'I heard that,' says Jimmy. 'Now you come to mention it, I think I might just stick to Pearl, who gives me a good working over and asks for nothing in return but a plate of fried chicken and a Red Stripe.'

'I'm sure Miss Taylor will be heartbroken,' says Noël.

'She has her Dick,' says Jimmy, waving his hand and walking away with a swagger. 'She'll get over it.'

A bird flies past the window. Noël files his thumbnail on a matchbox. He wipes his sunglasses on the crinkled hem of his shirt.

'Too much talking,' says Patrice, taking a sip of his beer.

'It seems I can't get away from it.'

'Do they talk a lot in England? I've heard the English people never speak their mind.'

'This one does,' says Noël. 'But I know how to précis.'

'I can't wait to see London.'

'You can't?' Noël raises his eyebrows. 'Wrap up warm. Have your mother knit you a very thick muffler.'

'You make me laugh, Boss. You say London is cold, but you also live in Switzerland where a man might turn into an icicle.'

'It's a beautiful place,' says Noël. 'A little like a chocolate box, but I'm happy there.'

'Because it's beautiful?'

'Because it's more than fucking beautiful and the tax man isn't a thief.'

Nodding, Patrice folds his arms, narrows his eyes and seems to consider the situation. 'It's certainly a worry, Boss. When I make my fortune, I'm going to need a very good money man to sort all that tax business out.'

'Talking of money, do you think my tab will stretch to a very large whisky?'

'I think,' says Patrice, 'it might stretch to two.'

# 3

H E SLEEPS for a couple of hours, wakes, then sleeps again. A dream. A memory. A long sandy beach, darkening with rain. Gulls hover, screaming. The sea swallows the rocks. It roars in a green-grey semicircle. The waves look like walls.

Noël stares at the horizon, shading his eyes from the wind. He wonders if the black moving object might be a ship, crammed with soldiers on their way to France. He can feel his teeth chattering. Someone slaps him on the shoulder. He turns.

'They say it's going to brighten.' It's Philip Streatfeild, Noël's new friend. Noël is fourteen, Philip thirty-five. Philip is well connected, an artist; bohemian. Noël's mother heartily approves of their friendship. She's allowed her son to join Philip on a road trip to Cornwall, where the air is fresh, briny, and as she will carefully explain (as she invariably has to), *'Noël has been suffering with his chest.'*

Noël grins. He can see the promised sunshine peeking through the clouds. He lifts his open hands towards it.

'We'll have tea,' says Philip, 'then we'll see about the painting.'

In their favourite tea-shop, Philip orders cocoa and Chelsea buns for Noël and three other young friends. They gape at the sea through the large picture window. Noël and the other boys wolf down the buns, while Philip sits languidly, smoking an Egyptian cigarette, legs crossed, revealing showy coloured socks slipping down his ankles.

The cove is empty, the sand drying in long ragged patches. Here, the boys run hollering, dancing with knots of tatty seaweed in their hair, throwing the strips of bladderwrack around their puny shoulders like pungent wet stoles. The blond boy trips about like his older sister, Claire. 'Of course I'll teach you the foxtrot! Heaven knows, I'm quite a sensational trotter!'

Stepping out of their cumbersome clothes they feel the freedom and joy of the elements. What a sensation! Noël, unabashed and exhilarated, becomes the leader of this cavorting trio of naturists, until Philip throws him a crushed white shirt, saying it might look rather good in the picture.

The boys are naked but for Noël's white shirt. They stand on an outcrop of rocks with a view of *la mer*. Noël can hear Philip breathing. The scratching of a pencil. His shoulders are aching, the back of his neck feels tight. He's good at standing still, but he longs to leap into the frothing water, to dance, to forget all the grim hopeless news about battlefronts and killing. He remembers a German boy he once met in a Corner House, a small ginger sapling eating sardines on toast.

A breeze ruffles Noël's shirtsleeves. A sharp piece of stone presses into his heel. A boy to his left starts sneezing, then laughing, and now it's no good at all because the boys are corpsing, and Philip starts lecturing, until the weather turns again, and they dash into a cave, blanketed, watching the sky change from blue into lead.

The rain wakes him. It hammers on the rooftop. When he glances at the window the world is full of water, the colours are vibrant; if he stretches his neck he can see the pink flowers dropping with the weight of it.

Patrice has his breakfast tray. 'Like England?' he says, setting it down by the bed and nodding at the weather.

'No,' says Noël. 'It smells different.'

Eating his scrambled eggs, he can already see the

explosions of blue dazzling through the rainclouds. In the Caribbean the rain comes pounding like a magazine of bullets, then it disappears, or stays with a deafening alacrity. There is no endless grey monotony. No freezing gunmetal drizzle. Nothing in between.

In England the rain had often stopped play. Large canvas sheets had covered tennis courts. Picnics were quickly abandoned and the contents of the heavy wicker basket had been eaten inside the car where they'd been grateful for the brandy and the Thermos flask of coffee, the warm running engine, knee blankets and copious cigarettes.

Rain changed the mood of the theatre. Halfway through Act One, women were still shaking out their dress sleeves, worrying about their make-up, their flattened hair, the wet ride home. Empty matinee seats would look like lost teeth. Programmes would melt. Someone would always miss their cue. At the interval, Noël would sit in his thickest plaid dressing gown wondering if the audience would return from their trip to the tea bar, the White Hart, or would the rain send them scuttling into the wide dry mouth of the Tube?

At Firefly the gardens are steaming. The air is redolent, like a stroll around a hothouse at Kew. Noël lies outside, stretched in his shorts with the sun in jagged lines across his squashy marbled thighs. He counts the bruises on his shins (nine). He watches a small green bird pecking at the swimming pool.

'I was thinking about the reference, Boss,' says Patrice, who has helped himself to an abandoned slice of toast. 'Would you have time to write it now? Please?'

Noël rubs his eyes. He has all day to write letters. With the air now clear and the sunshine so fiery, he wonders why anyone in their right mind would want to leave this tropical climate, to change their lightweight clothes for woollens, thermals, and damp gabardines.

'Do I have to?' he breathes.

'I will go and fetch some paper,' Patrice tells him, wiping toast crumbs from his lips. 'Some paper and an envelope.'

Noël can feel his nerves tightening. He pictures the hotel in Piccadilly and the slow grinding traffic. He can feel a gust of London air biting the back of his neck. From the corner of his eye he can see Patrice moving around the small glass dining table, arranging the headed sheets of paper, a stack of matching envelopes and the good black pen.

'Everything for your convenience, Boss, if you'd like to step inside.'

Grunting, Noël makes a show of closing his eyes,

of settling his hands and lowering his chin for yet another one of his naps. He can hear Patrice sucking air through his teeth, saying that his cousin Joe is a very lucky man. Not twenty-five years old and he is going to London, England, selling records. It is his dream come true, and though Patrice believes in dreams, he also believes you have to help them on their way. You have to apply yourself.

'Like Charles, Boss.'

'Who?'

'My old neighbour, Mr Charles. You painted him once.'

'I did?'

'A very good painting of him fishing in his little white shorts. Anyway, he wanted to be a chauffeur, even though he couldn't drive. He saw himself in a cap driving important people around the island. He took lessons from Francis. You remember Francis, Boss?'

'No.'

'You painted Francis also, totally naked, standing by your swimming pool – a very generous likeness. Well, Francis was good at giving his driving lessons, and Charles is now wearing his smart black cap, with gold braid trimming, and he drives an American car for the Coruba Rum Company's big shots. Now it's my turn.'

When Noël opens his eyes the sunlight is dazzling. 'How old are you, Patrice?' he asks.

'Twenty-two.'

'I'll give you driving lessons. We could start tomorrow, first thing.'

Patrice shrugs. He isn't interested in driving and cars are too expensive. Anyway, he's done all his research. In London they have buses. Red buses. Or the underground railway. The Tube.

'They also have racism and bigotry,' says Noël. 'Have you thought about that?'

'Brixton is just like Jamaica.'

'Yes, I've heard it's very picturesque.'

'You mean you have never seen Brixton, Mr Coward?'

'Whenever I'm in town, I usually tell my driver to take the scenic route.'

'But you will make an exception to visit Joe and Patrice? I'll leave you the address. You, and Mr Payn, and Mr Cole, will be welcome any time, day or night.'

'That's a very generous offer. I'll tell Lord Olivier he needn't bother airing out his guest room.'

Patrice nods. He wraps his fingers into knots. 'The letter?' he says, looking towards the house. 'It can be very short. It won't take five minutes, Boss. Really.'

Noël doesn't move. Sighing, Patrice unknots his fingers and clasps his hands loosely behind his back, until eventually he half-heartedly picks up a few sodden flower heads and throws them into a rubbish sack. He circles the swimming pool whistling what can only be described as a funeral song.

'Oh for heaven's sake, Patrice,' says Noël. 'Shut the fuck up and I'll write the letter later.'

Patrice stops. The flower in his hand is losing all its damp petals. 'Really, Boss? Today?'

Noël nods.

'You promise?'

'Cross my fucking heart and hope to die.'

Noël sits at the dining table, panting a little. He presses his fingertips into the glass. The room is small, the walls a blue wash, the carpet a dirty shade of crimson.

'Would you like to eat lunch now, Boss?'

Noël lights a fresh cigarette. His stomach feels tight. He can't remember his breakfast. 'I'll have something light,' he says. 'How about a salad?'

Resting his elbows on the table, Noël can hear Patrice moving around the tiny kitchen. He thinks about food. The summers of blackberries. Ices. Fools. The winters of steak and onions. Lamb's liver. Brisket. As a child he'd been allowed to stand on a chair to stir the Christmas pudding. He is not averse to Caribbean cuisine, but his favourite meal in Jamaica is plain beef sausage and mash.

'Here you are, Boss. Salad.' Patrice holds a plate of cold meat and chopped greenery.

'That was bloody quick.'

'I told you I was speedy, Boss. You can put that in the letter. You can time me! And look, I still have all my fingers.'

'Well set them to good use and remove all this literary paraphernalia, it's putting me off my lettuce.'

Nudging the paper to one side, Noël tries to find the cruet. The salt looks grey. The pepper pot is empty. Begrudgingly, Patrice moves the typewriter to the other end of the table and covers it with a teacloth, then he stands for a minute, tapping his fingertips over his thighs.

'Would you like a little music, Mr Coward?' he says. 'In large hotels they often have a pianist. They say it helps with the digestion.'

'You play the piano? You kept that very quiet.'

'No, Boss.' He slides his hands towards his hips. 'But I play a mean 45.'

Noël grins. A piece of fatty ham impaled on his fork starts flapping. 'Spin me a disc, Daddy O!'

Patrice winds his way around the furniture and out into the kitchen where he keeps his own stack of records in the pantry.

'My choice,' he says, blowing flour from the vinyl. 'My record.'

45

The record Patrice chooses to click onto the turntable is 'It Mek', by Desmond Dekker and the Aces. As Noël starts to grimace, Patrice dances. He moves like a water snake, ribcage rippling, fingers clicking over his shoulders, then down past his waist. Noël can feel his hands trembling, his frayed nerves flying like static. The music grinds to a stop. Patrice stops. It's over.

'I see you have great talent,' says Noël, as Patrice bends with the verve of a gymnast to lift the record from the player.

'Waiters are slinky creatures. How was the salad?'

'Remarkably tasty.'

Grinning, Patrice carefully slips the record into its stiff cardboard cover, then he goes to find a dishcloth. 'I will clear and wipe down, Boss. We don't want no tomato pips sticking to the envelope.'

'Don't bother rushing,' yawns Noël. 'I'm off for a little lie-down.'


Siesta. A crumbling public lavatory not far from Leicester Square. This less than salubrious public convenience has appeared in his dreams on and off for forty years, though he has never visited it, never seen it, and perhaps it doesn't exist.

A cold tap drips into the rust-stained bowl of a sink. A metal sign reads: Germs Spread Diseases.

There is the usual cracked pissoir (empty) and three stalls, two of which have their doors firmly closed. When he tilts his head he can see three pairs of workmen's boots. Two are sharing a stall, the other set of boots stand close to the partition. Noël looks down at his own shoes. They're too clean. Too Jermyn Street. He wishes he'd muddied them up.

Before another character can make his ill-timed entrance (it has happened) Noël dives into the open stall and locks the door behind him. For a moment he listens to the grunting and panting, the banging of the wall, which rattles so hard the lavatory paper starts unrolling from its holder like something you might throw at a newly christened liner. Eventually, he stands on the lid and peers over. The men are wearing donkey jackets. Jeans bunched around their wide oily ankles. He watches the sucking, the jerking and thrusting. He listens to the sounds from the last invisible booth; another voyeur with his cock out.

When he wakes his penis is shrivelled – unlike the old days when the dream would have him writhing in the bed sheets. His flaccidity depresses him. It feels like a bereavement. An unnecessary loss.

Patrice still hovers around the newly washed edges of the dining table. He flicks a duster over QWERTY. He puts a sheet into the roller. He pulls it out again.

Noël can feel his fingers twitching. He has to find something to do with his hands. 'Could you get my things from the studio?' he asks. 'And the letter . . .'

'Yes, Boss?'

'I'll think about the wording while I'm painting.'

'Excellent idea, Boss!'

Noël bows his head, clenches his teeth and smiles. Whistling, Patrice sets up the easel.

'Stop it,' says Noël.

'Stop what? You don't want to paint any more?'

'The whistling. Your whistling. It's really fucking getting on my nerves.'

Patrice tightens the screws of the easel in silence. He brings out the paintbrushes, palettes, and the new tubes of paint. They face the scrubby part of the garden, the grass scorched like stubble in parts. There is nothing to suggest the earlier downpour, here everything looks parched, almost toasted. Finally, Patrice reaches for the unfinished painting. Noël hasn't seen it in months.

'Trees, Boss?' says Patrice.

'They were going to be people,' Noël tells him, fumbling in his pocket for his lighter. 'I was rather good at people, once upon a time. Now I'm no good, I've changed them into trees. What do you think? It's my touch-and-Gauguin period.'

'It's very good, Boss. Very sunny. Did you ever paint in London?'

'I did a little bit in Kent.'

'Is Kent near to London, Boss?'

'Well,' he says, 'it's nearer than it used to be.'

After covering his hand with a small plastic bag (he's allergic to the paint), he squeezes a tail of magenta. The gauze on the window shifts slightly in the breeze. He wonders when he started the painting. He narrows his eyes; it seems the view has changed completely and he'll have to make it up. Wrinkling his forehead, he concentrates on the flower petals, which are now the colour of overripe tomatoes. With each small brushstroke he pushes everything from his head, the donkey jackets, his unwilling penis, the humming sound that fills his head and might be something mechanical. The letter.

*The letter.*

'When you've finished your painting and you've had a good think about the wording, Boss, perhaps we could go inside? I've wiped the area clean and I've put a new sheet of paper in the roller. And if you are tired, Mr Coward, I'll type the letter myself, and you'll only have to sign it with your autograph, which if you would allow me use of the fountain pen, I could make the perfect likeness.'

'My autograph is usually written by Mr Cole.'

'My Noël Coward is almost as good as his.'

For a moment Noël feels breathless. Giddy. Sitting on the stool he wonders if he'll have the strength to lift the brush again, to dip it into the paint daubed around the palette. It all seems such a bother. Today his on-off painting looks out of focus, like a wet Polaroid.

'All right,' agrees Noël. 'Later.'

He pauses at his desk. He looks at the papers. The crossings-out. The stop-start meanderings of dialogue and prose. His fingertips trail across the fat blue paperweight, three miniature starfish trapped inside the glass. His pen pot is stuffed with pencils, biros, and gold-plated Watermans. *The Concise Oxford Dictionary* is open at D, but he's too far away to see 'damask' or 'danger'. Taking a few steps back he rubs his forehead and studies the desk more closely. Something has changed. Shifted. He feels slightly panicked.

'You all right there, Boss?' says Patrice, coming up behind him.

'What's happened to the desk?'

'Nothing, Boss.'

'Nothing? Are you sure?'

Patrice tells Noël that it looks the same to him, though of course the typewriter is missing. 'I put it on the dining table, Boss. Would you prefer to write the letter sitting at your desk? Should I fetch it?'

'Not now, Patrice.'

He does remember the typewriter sitting on the table. There was a teacloth. He can picture the covered machine, a white lump pushed at an angle, the skew-whiff sheets of paper. He thinks of other times he has sat around the table, hacking at soft-boiled eggs, sticky piles of rice, wet cling peaches. He's opened bottles of wine. Played footsy. Rummy. Canasta. He's discussed fledgling actors, contracts, hotel bills. He can remember whole snatches of conversation from this time last year. *'We were stranded at the airport, we had to lie across the chairs, thankfully Hester had her mink, but we were terrified to sleep in case the bloody coat was stolen.'* *'I tried following the recipe, but my fudge looked more like canine diarrhoea than anything you'd want to slip between your lips on purpose, and for pleasure.'* *'Tired as we were, and we were bloody tired I can tell you, I quickly became Noël Coward and Judy was Dorothy Adorable. We're show people. Always were. Always will be.'*

There had once been ants in the butter dish. A gift wrapped in blue tissue and secreted between a pineapple and an unripe mango. He can remember all sorts of things. At the click of his fingers he can be at the Phoenix opening telegrams. He can hear the thud of the hooves at the races. Dialogue. A woman with gold-coloured hair is applying his make-up. He can see himself icing cakes in his small New York apartment. When was that? 1950 something.

Noël sits on the veranda with a glass of iced tea. The ground is dappled. A swirling flock of Jamaican starlings fly out to sea and form an almost perfect circle. He looks at the specks of paint on his shorts. They feel like cake crumbs. What happened to the painting? Has he finished it?

Patrice is inside, typing – presumably with one finger.

'I can hear you sulking,' says Noël, when his head appears at the window.

'Dear Manager . . .'

'Don't you have a name?'

'Manager.'

'But you do need a name,' insists Noël.

During the war he had walked through cramped hospital wards, where the wounded were recovering. They were sombre, sobering places. The men would call him Captain Coward, and though he'd only ever fought on celluloid, he hadn't put them straight, he'd nodded like a captain, smiled and shaken their hands; it would have been too rude to correct them. Walking between their tight iron beds, lighting cigarettes for those who couldn't manage it, he had reeled off their names like a register. Harry, Bill, Walter. 'How are you, Tom? Better?' It was a knack he had. The men had been impressed and had talked of it for weeks. 'He remembered me! That brave Captain Coward knew my name!'

'I'll make some enquiries,' says Noël. 'It's the little things that make all the difference. Names are important. They're a gift.'

Patrice steps out of the doorway. 'You mean like Coward?' he says.

'Don't be fucking impertinent.'

'Coward and Payn.'

'Well, just thank God I named Mr Cole myself.'

Patrice moves closer. 'You named him, Boss?' he says, scratching the back of his neck. 'Like his father? Like a preacher on his christening day? Like a dog? Did he not come with a name? Was he nameless?'

'Mr Cole Lesley was known as Leonard Cole, and Leonard is a name I simply can't abide.'

'So you fixed it?'

'He didn't say no. He was quite enthusiastic.' And Noël can see Coley standing in a tired mackintosh all those years ago. He's holding a letter of recommendation in his brown leather gloves. He can type. Valet. He can cook 'to some degree'. 'Nothing fancy required,' Noël tells him. 'A small late supper after the theatre. A little eggy something on a tray.'

53

'I am given to believing that the plantation owners renamed their slaves for their own satisfaction,' says Patrice. 'My great-grandmother was known as Blossom, when her real name was something else entirely.'

'Blossom? How very unfortunate. Was the woman particularly bovine?'

Patrice sits on the steps. He folds his arms. 'And do you know my name, Mr Coward?'

'I've been calling you fucking Patrice for the last three years, so now I expect you're going to announce yourself as Patrick, the ubiquitous Winston, or don't tell me . . . Leonard?'

'No, Boss. Fucking Patrice it is. Patrice Devan Raymond Autry Keenan Ramsden Clarke.'

'You sound like a shopping list. I'll have a box of Keenan Clarke and half a pound of Devan.'

'I was named for my uncles,' says Patrice, 'and every one of them a useless bag of shite, though my Uncle Raymond was all right, until he got killed falling from the roof of the Myrtle Bank Hotel.'

'Then perhaps as a mark of respect you should avoid the hotel trade altogether?'

'It wasn't the hotel, Mr Coward, it was the ganja.'

'I don't approve of weed.'

'You don't approve of weed, Boss?' Jumping to his feet and waving like a mango boy on market day, Patrice

54

says Jamaica is full of it, that half the wispy clouds sitting in the sky are probably made from its sweet intoxicating smoke. 'Can't you see it, Boss? It's why we walk with such a sway and sashay, and though it has plenty to recommend it, the sun, the rum, my mother, Jamaica is an island I want to fly from, I want to see more of the world, to escape for a while. Won't you help me to escape? To fly away, Mr Coward, Boss? Please?'

'Oh for fuck's sake, stop whining, just write the sodding letter and have done with it.'

'Really? Now? Should I bring the typewriter outside? I don't mind. I don't need a table. I could sit by your chair and type it very nicely on my knees.'

'On your knees, eh? Bring the machine outside, quick smart. There's nothing like a man tapping his Corona.'

Patrice leaps inside with the sort of gazelle grace Noël hasn't seen since he visited Sadler's Wells. Grinning widely, he reappears with the typewriter and a small stack of paper which he traps beneath a jagged piece of coral, before sliding one into the roller. 'Dear Manager . . .'

'Dear Sir,' says Noël.

Pursing his lips, Patrice replaces the paper. 'Dear Sir,' he says. 'Now what?'

'Now you need to recommend yourself,' says Noël. 'You need to big yourself up.'

'I do?' he frowns.

'Most certainly.'

Noël is suddenly thirsty, his mouth is dry, but to ask for a drink will seem churlish, and now he likes Patrice's naivety, his enthusiasm, the way he looks up, like a spaniel waiting for a knucklebone.

'"Dear Sir,"' says Patrice. '"I am writing to recommend to your service Mr Patrice Clarke . . ."'

'What about the shopping list?'

'Are you serious?'

'Deadly.'

Patrice replaces the paper again, screwing the old one into a tightly crushed ball and throwing it over his shoulder. '"Dear Sir, I am writing to recommend to your service Mr Patrice Devan Raymond Autry Keenan Ramsden Clarke, who has worked for me these past three years."'

'Very good,' says Noël, flapping the back of his hand. 'Carry on.'

'"He is loyal, dedicated, and extremely hardworking."'

Noël gives a wry, crooked smile. 'To a point.'

'"I am certain he will be a great asset to your world-famous hotel,"' says Patrice, '"where I have stayed many times."'

'And had a great many adventures.'

'You're putting me off my stride, Boss.'

'No I'm not, I'm helping.'

Gritting his teeth, Patrice tries to get to the end of it. '"I would be indebted if you could offer Patrice a position as a waiter, where his silver-service training would be put to good use."'

'Silver-service training?'

'By the time I get to England, Mr Coward, I will be a dab hand at it.'

'Dab.'

'Yes, Boss.'

'I miss him.'

'Who?'

'Dab.'

'Dab who?'

'His real name was Jack. No, John. He was an American.'

'Jack? John? Dab? Did you keep renaming him too?'

Noël lets his chin fall onto his chest. His mouth feels dry but he can taste whisky and Martini. Cognac and champagne. 'Of course he was a drunken little shit towards the end of his life, and the real Jack had gone a long time ago, but sometimes he comes back to me, the way he was, the charm he had, that . . . oh, I don't know, he had that buoyancy Americans seem to have, that confidence.'

'And was he handsome?' asks Patrice.

'God, yes.'

'Is that enough, Boss?'

'Well, it certainly helps things along.'

'I meant the letter. Should we yours sincerely now?'

'It's faithfully,' says Noël. 'And yes.'

# 4

PULLING THE door of his parents' lodging house behind him, he can already taste the cold bitter snow that starts to fall in dribs and drabs before he's reached the corner of Ebury Street. He pulls his scarf tighter. Occasionally, the pavement slips beneath his shoes making his heart drop into his stomach. The milkman, his cart now empty, lifts his gloved hand towards Noël, though the man sits with his head down, his leather cap dusted with fine white flakes, his horse moving stoically through the traffic.

Noël feels light. He feels like something blowing down the pavement, a play script perhaps, or a flyaway ticket. Yesterday was his twenty-fifth birthday. Last night his play, *The Vortex*, moved from its small Hampstead theatre (an ex-drill hall no less!) into the great West End. The evening had been an enormous success. The house was tightly packed. The play was so well received – for all its scandalous content – it seemed the audience didn't want to budge from their standing ovation, staying long after the curtain had dropped and Noël had wiped the greasepaint from his face.

Later he'd sipped champagne in his dressing room, receiving praise and adoration from his well-heeled guests. Outside, the crowds were pressing closer, whistling through their fingers, and shouting for a glimpse of their newly crowned idol. Standing in the cold they had called out his name, cheering when he'd finally appeared. They had proffered their programmes for his signature. He had been slapped on the back, his hand shaken so many times, his bones might have turned into jelly.

Now, manoeuvring into Sloane Square, he brushes shoulders with the mass of muffled office workers, women picking their way carefully through the slush, trying to keep their boots nice. Some of them look at him, shyly, lifting their eyes from the hazards of the pavement. For a moment he stops at the window of a Fine Swiss Confectioner, and the reflection in the glass shows that something about him has changed.

Avoiding a river of ice, Noël steps into an omnibus, shoulder to shoulder with yawning men, on their way to stamp bonds or dictate letters, to sell groceries, postal orders or machine-stitched shoes. Shuffling forwards, giving himself space to light a cigarette, Noël feels safely cocooned between their damp-smelling overcoats and leather-patched tweed.

Walking towards Leicester Square his thoughts turn to the other cast members, the friends and hangers-on from the night before. There'd been a birthday cake. He can see rows of empty bottles, popped corks, tattered buttonholes and pink bleary eyes. He assumes that most will be sleeping it off, and though he'd quaffed plenty of champagne, staying out until the small hours, he's never felt more awake or alert in his life. He smiles at passers-by. Doffs his hat at strangers. He giggles like a child at the Christmas windows with their elves in felt hats and the dancing mechanical robins.

On Oxford Street he steps into a small steamy café, where he orders tea and scrambled eggs, sitting at a table in the window. The snow seems to make London smaller. The green oilcloth floor is swimming with watery footprints. The tables are filling, newspapers are rattled, plates of bacon and eggs are produced from the kitchen, a small noisy space, hidden from view by a red gingham curtain. 'Might I have another sausage?' A man holds out his plate like an overgrown Oliver Twist. 'They seem an awful lot smaller than they used to be.'

Watching people passing by the window, Noël wonders if any of these frozen grey spectres were at the Royalty last night. His eyes follow them as they move along in shoals, gloved hands carrying string bags, boxes, smaller gloved hands.

When he pays the waitress she tightens her eyebrows – two uneven kohl arches – and by the look on her face she might be about to ask if she knows him from somewhere. Didn't she seen his picture in yesterday's *Express*? But the woman says nothing, pushing his money into her sagging apron pocket, then saying, 'Goodbye, sir, and thank you,' before retrieving a stubby pencil from behind her left ear to take another customer's order.

Outside, his breath forms a thin straggly cloud. The snow has shuddered to a halt, the gas lamps are glowing, the shop windows are illuminated, and though the streets are murky there are bright Christmas lights and colourful displays. Soon the housewives appear, pouring from the trams, children grabbing at their coat-tails, dawdling at the windows, even in the cold. Noël sidles past them. He walks along the Charing Cross Road, stepping into Foyle's, where the heat knocks him senseless for a few long seconds, and a man halfway up a stepladder with a stack of books in his hands (Ivy Compton-Burnett) recognises this new sensation and almost topples backwards, dropping two of the volumes, which Noël deftly catches before they can blacken his eye.

'Mr Coward? I'm very sorry, sir,' the man stutters, his face turning crimson. 'Many congratulations.'

Noël says nothing, but he smiles and nods his head, passing on the books as he briskly takes his leave, as though he's grateful for the praise, but this happens every day and is nothing to remark upon. He finds the children's fiction, N, and his fingers play along the spines of *The Phoenix and the Carpet*, *The Story of the Amulet*, *The Railway Children*, before pulling out *The Enchanted Castle*, and he decides to buy another copy to keep inside his dressing room. The woman at the till is visibly trembling as she takes the book from his hands. 'Thank you so much,' says Noël, and it seems the woman would like to reply, to start a little conversation, but when she opens her mouth nothing comes out, and she only just manages a tight-looking grimace of a smile.

He walks down cobbled backstreets. He lets his eyes drift towards the upstairs windows of junk shops, photographic emporia and sleazy-looking bar-rooms. These windows are firmly closed against the elements, their inner sills holding wine bottles, pot plants, candlesticks. Women in velvet shrugs stand huddled in peeling doorways, lighting foreign cigarettes, their scarlet lips cackling and hooting. Noël can smell garlic, spices, the charcoal griddles of the small foreign restaurants. Voices pour from open windows, melodious, fast and exotic. A man with olive skin and dark flickering eyes appears from the shadows wearing a pea coat, his right hand in his pocket, his head leaning against the frozen brickwork. He eyes Noël up and down, and Noël eyes him back, his heart is drumming, but he makes himself move on.

In Covent Garden he buys a fresh buttonhole. 'What's your name?' he asks the flower girl.

'Annie, sir.'

'Well, Annie,' he says, pressing some coins into her hand, 'have a very good day, sell lots of flowers and do keep moving before the frostbite sets in.'

Exhilarated, he bounds towards Waterloo Bridge for nothing other than the view, glancing towards the dome of St Paul's and across to Big Ben, whose shivering black hands tell him it's almost 10 o'clock. By the time he reaches the Royalty, the sky is starting to clear. At the corner of Dean Street and Shaftesbury Avenue, he walks slowly towards his name – those ten shining black letters. He thinks about his typewriter and the very first time he had tapped out the words: 'The Vortex. A Play in Three Acts'. Lighting a cigarette he watches a crowd of girls pushing towards the box office, a man posting last night's notices on the board: SOME RETURNS AVAILABLE.

'Tea, sir?'

'Tea would be lovely, thank you.'

'Biscuits?'

'A few Bourbon creams would be nice.'

His dresser has already seen to his costumes, the dress suits, pyjamas, the pale silk dressing gowns. He has arranged the bottles of Chanel and Floris cologne across his marble washstand and has sorted through the post, the small white envelopes in stepping-stone stacks across the table, alongside parcels, flowers, a case of Moët, truffles from Fortnum's, and a package from Hawes & Curtis, containing a dozen silk shirts and a necktie. There are hopeful invitations. Cards and telegrams. Fan mail.

Sitting at his dressing table he looks at his face in the mirror. He examines his profile. He presses his fingertips into his forehead.

'So this is London's newest star,' he says. 'Well, I am rather handsome – wouldn't you say so, Freddy?'

'Oh, yes, sir.' The dresser has arranged the biscuits into the shape of a flower and Noël's fingers dive for the nearest crispy petal.

'We've had calls all morning, sir,' Freddy adds, 'people asking for interviews and suchlike. The *Evening Standard* would like to photograph you at home – the playwright at work, that sort of thing.'

'Not at my bloody desk again,' Noël groans. 'I'll have

to think of something much more interesting than holding a fountain pen aloft with a slightly glazed expression, as if waiting for an idea to pop into my head. No, I shall tell the *Evening Standard* that I am a complete delinquent and my mind is a mass of corruption. I shall tell their reading public that I am never out of opium dens, cocaine dens, and other evil places, that my blood is awash with spirits and champagne.'

'Oh dear, sir.'

'Don't look so worried, Freddy. It will be excellent publicity.'

He reads a few of the letters.

Dear Mr Coward,

I think you are marvellous. Please could you send me an autograph and picture? I will keep it in my room.
    Sincerely, Ada Price

Dear Mr Coward,

I would do anything to meet you. Please let me know if this is possible. We could be very discreet. I have been told I look a little like Edna Best (especially my left side). I hope you like Edna Best. Reply to the above address before Thursday week if you can. I am going to Margate with my mother for a fortnight.

Forever Yours, Cynthia North

Dear Noël Coward,

I am the girl who waved and you waved back. I was wearing a black astrakhan coat. I have bought tickets for all my family (Friday Eve). Could you meet us backstage and act as if you know me? It would make my mother so proud. We wouldn't stay above ten minutes.

Yours, Delia Hatchet

'The House Full signs will be going out tonight.' The dresser appears with yet more flowers. Pale hothouse roses from Ivor Novello. Crinkled carnations from 'Lucy, a fan'.

'Mr Tennant wondered if you'd like to have lunch, sir?'

'I don't think so, Freddy. I'm going for my nap.'

'Should I wake you if he calls? Or should I tell him you're not in?'

'Freddy, you know my naps are sacred. If *God* calls, tell him I'm not in.'

\* \* \*

Noël wakes in his bedroom in Firefly. The room is stuffy. The fan is moving in grinding slow motion. He rubs his sticky eyes. He can hear the crickets chirping. He feels heavy. Damp. He pulls the sheet away. Closes his eyes. Sleeps.

His five-minute call. Noël steps into the wings feeling somewhat deflated. They're well into the run and the audiences are listless. They rustle sweet wrappers. Root through their handbags. They look towards the exit signs, squinting at the hands ticking on their cheap Woolworth watches.

'We need help. Listen to that, I can hear them yawning from here,' Noël mouths, but then he can't help noticing the American sitting rapt in the centre of the stalls.

'How do you know he's American?' whispers Mollie Sim, who's playing Clara Hibbert.

'By his collar,' says Noël. 'Don't you notice anything?'

The man has shiny black hair and a chiselled film-star profile. His teeth are porcelain perfect. At the end of the play his applause is so enthusiastic that Noël and the entire company bow in his direction. When he appears backstage with a mutual friend, Noël can hardly string a coherent sentence together. Drinks are poured, and in less than ten minutes the

American (already taking his leave) has invited the actor to lunch.

'When?' asks Noël, trying not to sound too enthusiastic.

'When you're next in the States,' says the man, or 'Jack' as he's introduced himself, with all the confidence of a moneyed Ivy Leaguer. 'You are coming to the States?'

'Of course.' Noël grins. 'It's my favourite place in the world.'

Noël can feel himself slipping. He keeps losing his concentration. He examines himself in the mirror, patting the outskirts of his twenty-five-year-old eyes with a pungent cold cream. He tries the blue silk scarf. The green. He kicks the stage manager. Then he kicks the rear tyre of his new Rolls-Royce. 'I've had it with England,' he boils. 'I want to move on.'

'Move where?' asks one of his fawning male coterie (a blond with nice hands and sea-green eyes). 'I had an aunt who went to China. Says it isn't all it's cracked up to be.' He giggles. 'It's supposed to be a joke. *China? Cracked?*'

Noël rolls his eyes. Shudders. He feels like throwing something heavy. These sycophantic men are getting on his nerves, acting like chorus girls, basking in his glamour. They are everywhere and however hard he tries, he just can't shake them off.

*Oh, say can you see by the dawn's early light.*
America! America! For weeks, months, he's been thinking of America, and now he's here with his mother, walking through Broadway, admiring the speed, the buildings that stretch from block to block, from asphalt floor to sky, their endless windows, glittering.

*The Vortex* opens in New York, in a thunderstorm; the sky cracks, the sidewalks are teeming with rain.

'It's a curse,' says Noël. 'Who'll come out in this?'

'They'll come,' the manager tells him. 'You'll see. They won't waste their three-dollar tickets on the rain.'

As soon as Noël steps onto the stage he knows he has them in the palm of his hand. The audience might be damp, their feet wet through and squelching, but these steaming New Yorkers are the most enthusiastic ticket holders he's come across in a long time. They lean forwards. Their mouths drop. At the curtain call, the place is in uproar.

'You see, Mother,' he says, pouring a glass of champagne, 'this New World is our greatest opportunity.'

And this New World offers Jack Wilson, who appears at the first matinee. The promised lunch is quickly arranged. They eat crayfish and lobster tails. They drink the finest chilled champagne. (Noël

70

blanches at the price tag.) Before the week is out, Jack becomes Noël's lover, producer, financial adviser, and Mr Coward's Number One fan.

Some time later: a garden. England. Jack pushes his hand into his inside pocket, pulling out an engraved silver cigarette case, a case Noël recognises as one of his own. It must be 1930 something. Dusk. They're sitting side by side looking at the croquet lawn, the mist rising from the edges, a mist blown in from Romney, because they're at Goldenhurst, Noël's large rambling farmhouse in Kent.

'You just can't stop yourself,' says Noël. 'And you're so fucking blatant with it too.'

Jack looks helplessly at the case. He presses a spring and offers Noël a cigarette. 'It's only a box, Poppa. A very little box.'

'You're such a kleptomaniac.'

'Do you mind?'

'Of course not, Raffles. I adore thieves. Always have done.'

'Really?'

'What's mine,' says Noël, 'is yours.'

'Always?'

Noël says nothing. He doesn't know what to say. He's still half in love. He'd like to believe in 'always', but with Jack he can't quite see beyond the end of next week.

'It's getting cold,' Noël says at last. 'I can hear the dogs barking.'

'Stay awhile,' says Jack. 'Look, the stars are coming out.'

But this one's going inside, Noël thinks. Still, he doesn't say it aloud – he often can't abide his own quick retorts. Instead, he touches Jack's shoulder. 'Don't be too long,' he says. 'Or you might be smitten with astronomy, and then it'll be telescopes and charts, and God knows what else.'

'Oh, I won't be smitten,' says Jack.

From an upstairs window, Noël watches his American jiggling his knees, pacing up and down the garden path. He holds the pilfered box and takes another cigarette. Hesitantly, Noël opens his bedside drawer, to see his best wristwatch glinting and ticking like a bomb. He sees all his jewelled tie pins. The ruby-studded cufflinks. He can feel himself blushing.

'Hello, Dab,' says Noël, later.

'What's that supposed to mean?'

'It's my new name for you.'

'I thought I was Baybay?'

'Well, now you're Dab.'

'I'm a fish?'

'No,' says Noël, loosening his collar. 'You're a fingerprint. You're my own petty criminal.'

'Then arrest me,' says Jack, holding out his hands. 'Go on. Cuff me. I insist on it.'

'Are you going to stay in bed all day, Boss?' says Patrice. 'Mr Payn is coming later, with a friend.'

'What friend?' Somewhere to the side of him, Noël can feel the shape of Jack Wilson. The strewn bed sheets are full of his impatience, smelling of hair oil, Burma-Shave, sweet-lime cologne. If he cranes his neck and looks at the floor, perhaps he'll find an abandoned White Arrow shirt? Black silk socks. American suspenders. 'Is someone here?' he asks.

'Not yet, Boss. Just me.'

Noël feels seasick. He drinks sweet tea. He tries to change the face of the American into someone he has never cared about. The men selling coconuts on the beachfront, the kite-maker, the boys along the roadside, their ever-blaring radios clinging like limpets to their shoulders.

'Is it 1971?' asks Noël.

'Yes, Boss.'

'He's been dead ten years.'

'Who's dead, Mr Coward?' Patrice is folding laundry. He keeps dropping things.

'Jack. Did you ever see Jack? No. You would have been a boy.'

'Did he come to Jamaica?'

'Oh yes. He often came here with his wife.'

'What?' Patrice stops. A pale yellow shirt is hanging from his fingers. 'He had a wife, Mr Coward? Your Jack Dab had a wife?'

'Oh, I was grateful to her really, these things happen you know.'

Noël takes another sip of his tea, scalding the tip of his tongue. He can hear Natasha admonishing Jack, but then she'd change her mind and play the great defender. Jack was her husband, her drinking pal, her handsome partner in crime. Who was anyone else to give their derisive opinion when she was wearing the wedding ring.

'We'd gone our separate ways a long time ago,' says Noël. 'Natasha was Russian. A princess.'

'A real princess?'

'Apparently.' Noël reaches for a cigarette. 'Love hurts, but it's curable.'

For a while, Patrice says nothing. He concentrates on the shirts. Then he presses down the lid of the laundry basket and sits on it. 'But you love Mr Payn?' he says.

'We've certainly had our moments,' says Noël.

'Where did you meet him?'

'If you must know,' says Noël, his eyes drifting towards the window, 'the first time I clapped eyes on Mr Payn he was fourteen years old and auditioning

74

for a revue. His audition was quite unforgettable. Not only was he singing "Nearer My God to Thee", he was also executing a rather well-timed tap dance.'

'And did he get the part, Boss?'

'Of course he got the part. For stamina alone I had to give the boy a job. We met again years later, and though our *amour* has faded and wandered, we've been close friends ever since.'

'He is a very loyal friend,' says Patrice.

'And loyalty goes a long way. Do you have someone, Patrice? A boy? A girl? A tourist?'

'Oh, I would never go jigging with a tourist, not after Mr Charles and the Canadian.'

'Charles fell for a Canadian?'

'Not exactly fell, Mr Coward. It was more like a train wreck. The Canadian gave Charles both lice and the clap, and the girl looked cleaner than a squeeze of Colgate toothpaste.'

'Looks can be deceptive.'

'I'm just glad I'm going to England, Boss, to make a different life.'

'Like your cousin. What's he called? Joe?'

'Yes, Boss.'

'Won't his family miss him?'

'His mama will be weeping and bawling,' says Patrice, 'but the mamas of his five children will be singing and dancing. He is not a good father,

75

Mr Coward, he has no interest in his boys, only in his music.'

'He has five sons?'

'Five that he knows of.'

'I thought he looked particularly fertile.'

'You never wanted children, Mr Coward?'

'Not for a second.'

'You have never loved a woman, Boss?' he asks, with a roguish glint in his eye. 'Not once? Not ever?'

Noël laughs. 'If you mean have I ever had sex with a woman, the answer is no. It would, I imagine, be like sleeping with a porpoise. Have I ever loved a woman? Perhaps.'

Patrice leans back, the basket wobbling as he drapes his arms across the window frame like a cormorant resting its wings. 'So you are a definite homosexual, Boss?'

'I like to give them a hand.'

'This part of the island is full of men who love men.'

'Does it bother you?'

'Of course not.' He shrugs. 'Why should it?'

A memory. A wood. England. 1912. Noël and the child-actor Philip Tonge have a knapsack each. These green canvas bags hang loosely by their straps, they bang into their hips as they walk. Philip's mother has provided hard-boiled eggs, a twist of salt, boiled ham, bread and butter, ginger cake and oranges; a flask of lemonade. They stroll swinging their arms, affecting characters, two country boys. Woodmen. Farmer's boys. A pair of sprightly goat-herders.

The trees are in full green leaf. The ground is a thick mossy carpet. Noël stands with his hands on his hips watching the rays of sunlight passing through the branches, catching the shadow of natural debris, like the footlights, dragonflies, the flight path of a bird.

Philip had thought to bring a tartan blanket. From past experience he knows the moss might look like the softest carpet, but it is always oozing with damp. He spreads it by a small stony stream. The boys roll their trousers to the knees, their ankles kissed by tadpoles, the water beading on their ice-cold skin. They slip and hold each other by the shoulders, balancing on the slimy flat rocks, colliding and laughing, until their heads draw closer, their hands start groping, and without pulling apart, they find the tartan blanket. It's Noël's first time. After an egg and a slice of ginger cake they try it all again. When Noël looks over Philip Tonge's shoulder, he can see a frog springing from the bank side; a splash as it leaps into the water.

Graham appears at lunchtime. Noël hasn't eaten his breakfast.

'He's lucky I'm vertical,' he tells Patrice. 'Who's he brought with him?'

'A woman, Boss.' Patrice, now wearing a necktie, for a reason Noël can't fathom unless their guest is Princess Margaret, kicks his espadrilles towards him, and he pushes them onto his feet, wearing them like flip-flops.

'This woman?' says Noël. 'Do we have a name?'

'I didn't catch a name, Boss.'

'Have you seen her before?'

'No, Boss, but she's a definite full-on beauty.' Patrice makes her curves with his hands.

'Be still my beating heart,' says Noël. 'Lead on.'

Through his sunglasses the outside world appears like something moving under cellophane. He sees Graham first, the woman has her back to him, but as soon as Noël waves, they both rise, scraping their chairs, already getting on his nerves.

'Hello, my darlings,' he says, arms akimbo, being all effusive, because Graham isn't introducing her, obviously feeling he has no need to introduce her, and Noël thinks he knows the woman's name, but if he isn't right, there'll be looks and knowing glances, and that will really piss him off. He's being kissed on both sides. There are murmurs of 'You're looking well,' and other inane responses.

The woman has honey-coloured skin, with a wrap

of black hair, pinned at one side with a lily. Her blue dress (which might be part skirt, part swimming costume), reveals three small moles and a ravine of heaving décolletage. She has twinkly gold sandals on her feet.

'Well, you look like something glowing,' says Noël, reaching for a drink. 'Did you walk up the hill?'

'Oh, I don't walk,' the woman tells him, amazed. 'I used to walk in Central Park, but when I looked across my shoulder I had a crowd of people following me. It really wasn't pleasant.'

'Who were they?' he asks, leaning forward. 'The fucking FBI?'

'No silly. Fans and photographers.'

Noël winces into his drink. So the woman is famous. Of course she is. Perhaps he should ask for her autograph? 'And how are you liking Jamaica?' he smiles, praying she isn't an illustrious lifelong resident.

'It grows on me by the hour. But I'm lost without my Pomeranians. They're staying with Dan and they're missing their mommy terribly.'

'And who could possibly blame them?' Noël grins, trying to think of all the Dans he's known and how they might be related to this dog-loving American beauty.

'I worry. You see, I've always been unlucky with my dogs. I lost two to rat poisoning, one to cancer, one to nothing in particular, and when we came to see you in Vegas we lost little Boo to a mail truck.'

'Poor Boo.' Noël tries to look his most sympathetic. He pulls his sunglasses down to the tip of his nose, hoping for just a little bit of help from Graham, but Graham is simply shaking his head and wallowing in the tragedy.

'And are you keeping well?' he asks.

'Don't believe everything you read in the papers,' she tells him, narrowing her eyes.

Noël can feel a pounding in his head, a pounding that might be from the vodka raining down on an empty stomach, but most probably comes from the effort of his probing conversation. 'Please do excuse me for a minute,' he says.

He finds Patrice setting a rather elaborate lunch table. He's used the best lace cloth. He's stuck an orchid into a vase. 'Who the fuck is she?' Noël hisses. 'Go and find out.'

Patrice looks up from his fussing. He breathes on the blade of a butter knife, before wiping it with a cloth. 'And how might I do that, Boss?'

'Be creative.'

'Can't you ask Mr Payn, Boss? Can't you take him to one side? Ask him straight out?'

'What's wrong with you, Patrice? Just get out there and do it!'

'Okay, Boss, okay, I'll do it,' he says, throwing down the cloth like a stroppy adolescent.

Noël stands in the shadows of the window, watching Patrice sidle up to the table, and after offering a bowl of peanuts (quickly refused) he pours another drink, and Noël can hear them laughing. The woman shakes her head. Patrice throws Noël a triumphant glance across his shoulder, and now he's on his way back with a swagger.

'Her name is Coral, Boss.'

'Coral?'

'Like that thing you find in the ocean.'

'I know what fucking coral is,' he says, but then the curtain rises and Coral isn't the elaborate marine deposit that the shops sell at exorbitant prices, she's a small-time movie actress married to a producer Noël once worked with, rich as Croesus, and she's only staying a couple of days, thank God, because from what he can remember she eats next to nothing, drinks like a fish, lies like a politician, and though he supposes that might be said of most of the actresses he has the pleasure of knowing, she seems worse, because in his far less than humble opinion, she hasn't any talent.

'What did Graham bring her here for?' he hisses. 'Bastard. And by the way, Patrice, I wouldn't go to too much trouble over lunch, our guest eats nothing but lettuce and those Swedish rye cracker things.'

Patrice looks disappointed as Noël shuffles back towards the table. His espadrilles make a thrumming, flapping sound. When the woman, Coral, pulls off her sunglasses, her eyes are a thin shade of blue.

Noël drifts while Graham talks about a shopping trip. He can feel the vodka tonic bubbling like Vesuvius in his stomach. The world looks slightly tilted but at least the panic has gone. The two of them are talking with great enthusiasm about engraved jewellery, hooded beach towels, and a Jew called Leonard Cohen. Turning his head, Noël sees Patrice standing on the steps. His feet are lost in a heat haze. He has a stiff white cloth folded neatly over his bent right arm.

'It looks like luncheon is served,' says Graham, getting to his feet.

'Oh?' says Coral. 'Are we eating?'

Although Noël loves Graham dearly, he wishes he'd take Coral home, because at this minute he would like nothing better than to eat his lunch alone, an omelette perhaps, or a beef salad sandwich, while flicking lazily through the *Gleaner*.

'The table looks smashing,' says Graham. 'I think Patrice is after promotion.'

'Promotion?' says Noël. 'Patrice is after leaving.'

'He's leaving?'

'Possibly,' Noël tells him, as Patrice appears

through the kitchen door, struggling with the plates, one of which he nearly drops. 'And then again, possibly not.'

Noël can see the beads of sweat sitting like glass in Patrice's wiry hair as he offers a basket of bread rolls, serving them with a pair of silver tongs.

'Just leave the basket,' says Graham.

'It's okay, Boss. Thank you, Boss, I'm fine.'

'Hell's bells,' Noël mutters, when Patrice returns to the kitchen for the wine, the label of which is shown to them all in turn, and they nod appreciatively, Coral telling Patrice to keep pouring as it looks so refreshing and such a rich ruby red.

'You don't expect to drink wine in Jamaica,' she says.

'What do you expect to drink?' asks Noël. 'Ginger beer?'

'Oh no,' she giggles. 'Rum punch. I heard everyone drinks rum punch.'

'I like rum punch,' says Graham.

Patrice looks upset. 'You wanted rum punch, Boss?'

'No, thank you, not now, the red wine is perfect.'

Bowing, Patrice leaves the room.

'He's trying his best, poor lamb,' says Graham. 'Whatever happened to, here you are, there you go, and just help yourself?'

Noël would like to disappear until the plates are quite in order and the food is safely on them. He can hear Patrice moving things. The creaking of his shoes. When he next appears he's brandishing a plate of something grey, surrounded by a fringe of rather limp lettuce leaves.

'What is this?' asks Graham.

'This is pâté, Boss,' he says, hovering at Coral's left shoulder with a knife, which he presses into the block as the whole pile wobbles and the pâté makes a squishing sound. 'Just the tiniest sliver,' she says, her mouth now pressed into a very tight smile. 'And might I have some lettuce?'

Graham tackles his pâté with such unbridled enthusiasm, spreading it over the bread, smiling with each bite, it seems he might be auditioning for a television commercial. By now Noël is ravenous so he gives it the benefit of the doubt, trying not to grimace, or to look too closely as he brings it to his lips, and is pleasantly surprised by the taste, if not the texture, which makes him think of junket. Coral pushes hers beneath her largest lettuce leaf.

'Does Vegas seem like a long time ago?' she asks. 'It feels like an age ago to me.'

'That's because it was an age ago,' says Noël, lighting a cigarette. 'It was 1957.'

'1955,' says Graham, 'and you must have been

that pretty little girl the management let in as a very special treat.'

She blushes. 'It's true,' she says, 'I was very young. The press called Dan a child snatcher, and all sorts of ugly names.'

'Poor Dan,' says Graham.

'You know, I think he rather liked it.'

Graham tries to keep the conversation going as their plates are cleared and clean ones are brought in their place. Noël's appears to have a smear of dried ketchup on the rim, which doesn't surprise him, and which he tackles head-on with his thumbnail.

'Of course,' says Graham, 'we had a splendid time, but the worst thing was the heat. The Desert Inn and all those other buildings were so well air-conditioned you almost forgot you were in Nevada until you stepped outside and your shoes became glued to the sidewalk.'

'Do they have sidewalks in Nevada?' says Coral. 'I never saw any sidewalks.'

Noël gives her a withering stare, forgetting he's removed his sunglasses, though Coral doesn't seem to notice, her face almost lost in a cloud of grey tobacco smoke.

'I wanted to see a cactus,' she says. 'Like in the cowboy movies. I made Dan drive me all over the place. And of course we went gambling. Did you go gambling?'

she asks, as Patrice appears with a plate of steaming chicken legs.

'When in Rome . . .' says Noël, thinking of the hoards of bespectacled middle-aged ladies, pulling the one-armed bandits as if their lives depended on it, sipping Coca-Cola through paper straws, their fingers reaching for their refreshments (sugary rolls, potato chips, crackers) like Tour de France cyclists as they continued in their quests for a waterfall of change.

'And were you lucky?' she asks.

'Oh, he's always lucky,' says Graham. 'He knows when to stop.'

'I had a hard childhood,' Noël tells her, with a woeful tilt of the head, 'which has given me a legacy for thrift.'

From the corner of his eye Noël can see Patrice struggling to hold a greasy chicken leg between the tongs, the drumstick swinging, his teeth sinking into his protruding bottom lip.

'I'll just use my fingers,' says Noël.

'I can manage, Boss. Thank you,' says Patrice, as the leg falls clattering onto the plate.

'Would you do it again?' Coral asks.

'If I'm feeling very weak, I usually have a bet on the St Leger.'

'Vegas! I meant Vegas! I'm sure you'd sell out, especially with your knighthood. You could even wear your medal. You do get a medal, right? We Americans love all that pomp and ceremony. You'd go down a bomb.'

'I'm sure I would,' says Noël. 'Still, I think I'll quit while I'm ahead.'

'I saw Judy Garland,' she says. 'Only two tables away. Dan said he knew her, but in the end he didn't. I wanted to get her signature, but Dan told me not to be so fawning, that I was embarrassing him, that I was always embarrassing him, and I should keep well away.'

'Judy was always charming,' says Graham, as a lump of potato falls from Patrice's spoon and lands in the centre of his plate. 'We miss her. We loved her very much.'

'Oh, you know everyone.'

'No,' says Noël. *'Everyone knows me.'*

They eat for a while in silence, chicken, potatoes, peppers, beans. Noël can see Coral pushing her food around, then he chooses not to look at her at all. He has a sudden recollection of the man in the pea coat. The dream had seemed so real and the man so familiar, Noël thinks if he put down his cutlery and stepped through the door, he might find himself in Soho, and if he retraced his steps, perhaps the man would still be there, his hand inside his pocket, his head against the wall. Waiting.

'Do you have plans for this afternoon?' asks Graham. 'I thought I'd take Coral shopping.'

Chewing on a piece of chicken, the image of the pea coat still at the front of his mind, Noël immediately thinks of a shopping trip as Harrods, Peter Jones, or Simpsons. He looks puzzled. 'Shopping?' he says, slowly lifting his head. 'But how?'

'How we always do it. We'll have the car. It's less than an hour and Coral will get to see more of the island. I thought I'd take her to Drummond's. It's a cavern of local arts and jewellery.' He turns to her. 'Of course the island has changed since we first came here in the fifties, but Drummond's is a gem, you'll love it.'

'We came in 1948,' says Noël.

'Did we?' says Graham. 'As long ago as that?'

'Didn't you once have a shop?' Coral asks.

'Of course not,' snaps Noël. 'Heavens.'

'We did have a shop,' says Graham. 'Designs for Living. It was for local people to sell their crafts, to train, to make a decent income for their families.'

'So you did have a shop.'

'I'm going outside,' says Noël, pushing back his chair. 'Please excuse me, I need a breath of air.'

'Are you feeling unwell?' asks Coral.

'Just a little hemmed in.'

'There's mousse for dessert,' says Patrice, his shirt

a little darker, his tie hanging crooked. 'It's chocolate. Milk chocolate, Boss. Your favourite.'

The flowers bounce in the trickle of a breeze. Noël sits on the edge of his seat, smoking, mesmerised by the pale sprouting stamens and the wide oily petals in twenty shades of red.

'Are you all right?' Graham appears, crouching at his side.

'Perfectly. Where's Carol?'

'Coral. She's in the bathroom. I thought you liked her. For goodness' sake, you told me to bring her to lunch.'

'I did? I must have been pissed. You must have been pissed.'

'Why?'

'You went and fucking believed me.'

Sighing, Graham gets to his feet, brushing down his trousers. 'It doesn't matter. We'll go after coffee.'

'What about tonight?'

'I'll have to take her to supper.'

'Could you spare Coley for an hour?'

'Of course, yes, I'll send him up at seven.'

The album feels warm in his hands. Musty. There are spots of dried glue. He sees lines of young men, naked but for the black and white towels pulled around

89

their waists, or thrown across their suntanned shoulders. They're laughing. Always looking for the camera. They're holding drinks and cigarettes. Sunglasses. Graham and Coley are everywhere. There are dinner tables, beaches, hammocks. Neighbours are standing by the piano, arms hanging around necks. No backbiting. Everybody smiling. Peter O'Toole with the worst hangover in the world, *Really, why won't you believe me? I've called an ambulance for far less than this*, stands with a hand across his clammy forehead as Noël tries to tempt him with another glass of booze.

'Patrice!' Noël shouts. 'Patrice!'

'Yes, Boss?' Patrice appears, dragging his feet. He looks beaten.

'I was going to ask for tea,' says Noël. 'Are you quite all right?'

'Yes, Boss.'

'Really?'

'No, Boss.'

'Sit down, put your feet up, and tell me all about it.'

Patrice slumps into the nearest chair. He seems to hang from the cushion, his hands almost trailing the floor tiles. 'I messed up, Boss.'

'Messed what up? What the fuck are you talking about?'

'Lunch, Boss. It was a complete disaster.'

'No, it was a jolly good effort,' Noël tells him. 'Unfortunately, the guest was rather difficult. She is not a great eater of food.'

Patrice, still wearing the sweat-drenched shirt, though the tie has been abandoned, breathes heavily, as if he might be sucking all the air from the room. 'The service was wrong. All wrong. I'll never get a job at the Ritz.'

'Look,' says Noël, 'I've eaten in restaurants all my life, and though I couldn't call myself an expert on the waiter side of things, I would say I was an excellent observer. I know a few rules of silver service. I could point out one or two things. Should we say, Sunday?'

'Boss?'

'Coral will have fled the island by then. I'll invite Graham and Coley. We'll help you out. What do you say?'

'I say, thank you, Boss.' Patrice slowly lifts his head. His eyes look wet as he smiles. 'I say yes, Mr Coward Boss, and thank you.'

'I had a dream about Jack,' says Noël.

'Jack Buchanan?'

'Oh, ha fucking ha.'

'All right. So was he good Jack, or bad Jack?' Coley sits beside him on the veranda. They're drinking the cocktails he's brought from Blue Harbour in a stainless-steel Thermos flask.

'Good and bad. The dream was all mixed up.'

'They usually are.' Coley nods wisely; he's a man who's come a long way from his days as an all-round valet, producing little eggy somethings on a tray.

'When I woke up, I missed him.'

'Well of course you did. That stands to reason. And how are you feeling now?'

'Christ!' Noël snarls. 'I don't need bereavement counselling, or whatever the fuck those American new-age quacks are offering these days. He's been dead for nearly a decade. Hell.' He shakes his head as if he can't quite believe it. 'Oh, you know all about Jack, you know I fell out of *grande amour* years ago, and then there was Graham, and all that other stuff, but in the dream it was as if everything had been erased. All the bad things. He was here. I'd only just met him. Mind you . . .'

'What?'

'He was still a fucking thief.'

They sit staring at the sea, the light glancing off the waves. The wide stretch of sky. Blue.

'How's the actress?' asks Noël.

'Coral? I think she bought Kingston. Her room is full of bags.'

'Does she think I'm going gaga?'

'Of course not, why should she?'

Noël circles his cigarette. 'Oh, because I didn't have the heart or the capacity to endure her presence with a painted-on smile and a sprinkling of *bons mots*. Because I left the table before we'd had dessert and I didn't give a shit. Oh, I don't know, I have the feeling I behaved like a dithering, grumpy old man, and she left here feeling hurt.'

Coley raises his eyebrows. He unscrews the flask and tops up their drinks. 'I'd be amazed if she felt anything. She seems rather armour-plated.'

'Actressy.'

'But we like actresses,' says Coley. 'Don't we?'

'Yes, and we couldn't do without them, but I'm getting sick of the egos. Sick of all the high maintenance required just to get them into the blasted theatre these days. The cars. The assistants. The "have you got a little basket for my doggy?" Not to mention the billing. Christ, let's face it, if they worked selling records in Woolworth's most of them would be shown the door in five minutes.'

'Though they might pull in a crowd.'

Noël grins. 'Can you imagine Liz Taylor in a BRI-Nylon overall selling 45s?'

'I'd buy one. So would half the population,' says Coley. 'Though I'd buy ten more from Mr Burton. Those pale searing eyes . . .'

'I can just see the manager wringing his hands. Will they, or won't they, show up?'

'She'll be gone in the morning.'

'Liz?'

'Coral.'

'Do tell her I said goodbye, and you'd better give her my love, for what it's worth. And no more visitors. Please.'

'I tried to warn Graham.'

'Since when has Little Lad ever listened?'

'Canapés, Boss?' Patrice stands with a tray holding saucers of cocktail sausages, cheese-filled peppers, and shiny crimped-edged pastries.

'My word,' says Coley. 'You're making an effort. We usually make do with a few bags of crisps and an olive.'

'He's doing very well,' says Noël, taking a pepper. 'And by the way, you and Little Lad must come to supper on Sunday. Patrice would like to practise silver service.'

'You want to be a waiter?'

'He's going to the Ritz,' Noël tells him. 'In London.'

'Good for you,' says Coley. 'I've always liked the Ritz.'

They eat something from each saucer. They grimace at the pastries. The sausages are stale.

'Did you do your walk today?' asks Coley, as a small green bird starts pecking at the crumbs now scattered at their feet.

'Honest answer: no.'

'Perhaps we should go now? While it's cool. Just for five minutes.'

'Five minutes,' says Noël, 'and not one minute more.'

Arm in arm they walk slowly between the trees. The crickets are singing, and they seem to attract a show of blue butterflies as Noël stops to grab his cardigan. 'This walking lark is always so much easier in Switzerland,' he says. 'Though you have to skirt around the mountains like a goat.'

'Mountains?' says Coley. 'Don't make me laugh.'

Five minutes pass. Then ten. They sit on a wall. Tonight the sea reminds Noël of blue denim jeans, the uniform of the young. He feels ancient. Heavy. He feels like a monument carved out of sandstone.

'You know, Coley,' he says, 'when Jesus wants me for a sunbeam, I'll be very glad to go.'

'Don't say that.'

'I expect I'm on His waiting list.'

'Look,' says Coley, holding out his hand, 'I've had a quiet word with the man upstairs, and I have it on very good authority that it isn't time for you yet.'

'I don't like looking foolish.'

95

'I know.'

They walk back in silence. Noël can feel his heart beating, he can hear its deep thumping, and it's something that he hates, because hearts aren't meant to be noticed, they're just meant to work. He hums. Humming seems to take the pressure away, and now all he can hear is the music in his head, the crack of his sandals, and Coley shifting gently to the side of him.

# 5

Patrice is going into Kingston for the morning. 'Isn't Kingston a little far for a morning jaunt?' asks Noël. 'And the roads are bloody terrible.'

'It'll be a long morning, but I need to go there, Boss. Should I get you some tea now?' he says. 'Coca-Cola? A beer? How about I cut you a sandwich?'

'I'll cut my own sandwiches today, thank you very much.'

'I'll not be away too long. I could get Mr Cole to come up. We could take you to Blue Harbour. I could call for the driver.'

'Oh for fuck's sake just go,' Noël tells him. 'Go on! Piss off! I really don't need another babysitter.'

A feeling of utter joy sweeps through him when the door clicks shut and Patrice disappears down the lane. Noël finds a straw hat, his oldest pair of shorts, and a shirt with the buttons conveniently fastened, so all he has to do is to push it over his head – though even this has him wheezing and panting.

When his breath slows down he finds himself sitting in a searing patch of sunshine. Reaching his arm across, and leaning on one elbow, he manages to push the sunshade open and the glare becomes a wide jade puddle which he finds very satisfying, though he might have done something to his shoulder. He rubs it. He looks across the table and realises that he's left his book inside. Fuck, damn and blast it, he thinks. It'll bloody well have to stay where it is.

Noël stares at the pool and itches to be floating. He's only just got himself dressed. It will take far too long and far too much effort for him to strip off, to lower himself in, and to scramble out again. Not to mention the drying and dressing. He tries to think of nothing. It's hard to think of nothing.

A swallow skims the water, it pecks and flicks at the droplets, fluttering its wings. Noël watches, fascinated. He hums a tune. He hums it again. It's a new tune. Perhaps the start of a new composition. Well, well, well! He has to smile. For months he hasn't been in the least bit creative – those few magenta petals being the very poor exception. He thinks of some lyrics, tapping his fingernails on the table. *Roses are red, birds can fly high, when you think of a heaven, you look at the sky* . . . He glances towards the open doors. The shadow of the piano. Would all the effort be worth it?

Drenched in sweat he sits on the piano stool. The top of the Bechstein is covered in silver-framed photographs. Here, Rudolph Nureyev nudges Vivien Leigh. James Mason stands behind a smiling Queen Mother. He lifts the lid and looks at the yellowing keys. Now he hasn't the slightest recollection of the tune. He sits and stares at his open mottled hands. The nicotine stains on his fingers. He could weep. Still, he might as well play something. As his neck drips into his soft open collar he manages a half-hearted rendition of 'Sail Away', all the time racking his brains. Birds? he thinks. Were there birds in it? Shit.

He sits for a while. He can't be bothered to move. Folding his arms across the lid he imagines his life a month or so from now. He'll have to dress in decent clothes. Don his good felt hat and proper lace-up shoes. Boots even. The public will be looking. He'll have to board a plane to New York and Geneva, and he hopes with all his heart he won't have to use the wheelchair again. The press are always looking for an angle. If he's in the chair he has to smile a lot. He has to keep his nerve. He'll tell them that the chair's sole purpose is to get him swiftly through customs.

They'll lap it up. Their headline: CHAIR-BOUND NOËL COWARD HEADS OUT OF THE MIDDAY SUN.

With an effort that sets him groaning aloud, he drags his flapping espadrilles towards the kitchen for a beer, trying to think of that thing he's left inside and would like to have outside. He takes the hessian shopping bag and fills it with packets of crisps, Bourbon biscuits, beer, a bottle opener, an empty notebook, a pencil and his book. When he reaches the chair, he feels more than pleased with himself. The book, he smiles. I have remembered the book.

After a few gulps of beer, he needs the lavatory. Hell. Why hadn't he felt the urge inside, when everything was convenient? With heavy breathing, puffing, panting, and yet another river of sweat, he makes it into the bathroom. He lowers himself onto the warm black seat. Fuck it, he thinks, wiping his forehead with a few sheets of lavatory paper, I could sleep here.


Limehouse, London, 1961.

An autumn evening. Mist and thick drizzle.

The Pilot. A public house usually frequented by river men, warehouse workers, bargemen and the like.

Busy, but not heaving.

Noël enters. He's wearing a reefer jacket. A muffler.

Buttoned into his coat is a small biscuit-coloured dog, a chihuahua crossed with something.

He orders half a pint of bitter. The barman, a young tattooed Elvis fan, thinks nothing of the old man who seems to be taking a while to sort out his change.

'Filthy evening,' says Noël.

The barman looks up. Shrugs. Says nothing.

Noël finds a seat by the grimy bow window. He pets his dog, who appears quite content buried between his thick coat and his sweater. Sipping his watery beer, Noël gazes at the advertisements for Guinness, Watney's, and Black Cat cigarettes. A man with oily fingernails asks him for a light.

'Filthy evening,' says Noël, holding out his lighter.

The man grunts. He looks at the end of his newly smouldering fag before quickly turning away.

Eventually, a man takes the opposite chair. He's wearing a jacket not dissimilar to Noël's (*sans* dog) and has a scrappy-looking scarf tied around his neck. He's about forty, with a wave of dark hair. His palms are mapped with dirt. He has a pleasant, roundish face, his eyes the colour of newly dried mud. Noël keeps quiet for a minute or two. He reads the notices. A lost wallet. A timetable. Something about a darts team.

'Nice dog,' says the man.

Noël opens a button and the dog pops out his head

like a wide-eyed jack-in-a-box. 'You like dogs?' he asks.

The man nods. 'We have a bulldog at home. I'd like another, but the missus won't let me.'

Noël laughs. 'Women, eh?'

'Thing is, she dotes on the bitch.' The man takes a gulp of his pint. He opens his packet of crisps and offers one to Noël.

'Thanks,' he says. 'I'll take one for the dog.'

'You working in Limehouse?'

'Of course not.' Noël shakes his head and smiles. 'Don't you know who I am?'

The man bends a little closer. Squints his muddy eyes. 'You're not a pal of Georgie's are you? He does know all sorts of people, what with his old man working in the shipping office.'

'I'm the man who wrote *Cavalcade*.'

'You did?'

Noël nods. 'Do you know it?'

'Is it about life in the military? I only tend to read the thrillers. Did it do all right? Did it make you any money?'

'It didn't do bad,' says Noël, getting to his feet and buttoning his coat.

'You off then?' says the man. 'Nice to meet you anyway, and good luck with the writing.'

The drizzle has turned into a fine sheet of rain.

The river is invisible. With his head down he moves towards the yard at the back of the pub. It's almost pitch-black. He can feel the dog shivering. Stepping further inside, he looks for signs of life. A glowing fag end. Surreptitious coughing. A low, cooing whistle.

When he opens his eyes he's lying on his bed. He has no recollection of leaving the bathroom. Did he sleepwalk? His shorts are damp and bunched around his aching knees. He looks at his alarm clock. Has it stopped? He squints at the hands, and though his vision is hazy he can see something moving. He pulls it closer to his face. Patrice has been gone for fifty-eight minutes.

He lifts himself up, has his usual dizzy spell, and thinks he'd better eat. He'll feel better after food. In the kitchen he leans over the sink and runs a glass of water. A fly starts hurtling itself at the rather colourful calendar (Jamaicans with fruit on their heads). He opens the fridge and lets the cool air waft across his body. The inside light trembles over slabs of cheese, a bar of milk chocolate and a bowl of giant tomatoes. He finds the butter and slices of the garlicky bologna he likes, then he goes hunting for the bread, which he sees wrapped in wax paper next to a greasy bag of truffle cakes. For the climate, the butter is remarkably solid. It tears the bread. When the sandwich is assembled most of its contents are peeping through the cracks, the lurid pink sausage like a nude caught between a pair of shredded curtains.

Taking his plate outside he's surprised to find the table still covered with the earlier debris. He wonders why no one has cleared it. The bottles of beer are warm. The biscuits have melted into one brown slab. The light has shifted, and the shady pool of jade is now wobbling over three stone plant pots and an abandoned bottle of Ambre Solaire. He sips the warm beer. Pulls his sandwich apart. Lights another cigarette.

The water takes him fully clothed. It buoys him up. Here he does not have to deal with the tired flabby weight of his body. Panting, he scrambles for the lilo and with one deft move he has it underneath him. His battered straw hat covers most of his face. It smells of salt and Kent.

He indulges in a daydream. A Jamaican boy in his early twenties is moving through Kingston. He's wearing a plain white T-shirt. Tight indigo jeans. He weaves between the crowds, hips first, shoulders rolling, like the models Noël has seen on the catwalks in Paris, or those burly (though strangely coquettish) sailors in port.

Occasionally the boy stops at a window and presses

his hand across his hair. He looks at the clothes on the rails. The leather belts with the huge gold buckles. Bracelets. The colourful nylon beach shorts.

Plaster madonnas line the window of Claude O'Connor's. Some of them are black. Posters fade in Jack Henry's. The Supremes. Temptations. A bikini scooter girl. The boy buys a Red Stripe and leaps onto a wall, sitting with his legs dangling, watching the world go by. He whistles. Noël can hear him. It's a Johnnie Ray song. '*Just Walking in the Rain*' . . .

'You going somewhere?' the man in the book shop asks. The boy is now inside the shop and hovering at the travel guides, his fingers tugging at the faded blue spine of *London, England*. He glances guiltily over his shoulder. He's only looking. Scanning the index for Brixton.

'You ever been to England?' the boy asks. The book shop is large but the stock is sparse, some of the shelves holding no more than half a dozen books, pulp fiction, horror, or trite religious verse. The travel guides are not extensive. From what the boy can see, they cover London, New York and Amsterdam. There are stacks of magazines, pads of cheap paper and tubs of sticky biros. A plastic snow globe shows a grinning Rasta Santa Claus with a spliff the size of his forearm.

The man grins. 'I went to England once,' he says. 'The longest three weeks of my life, *cha!*'

'You didn't like it?'

The man shakes his head. 'I was a baby. A pickney. Not ten years old. My uncle is still over there. Fool that he is. Works on the trains.'

'A train driver?'

The man has a little chuckle to himself. 'Nah. He just sweeps the filthy platforms. Cleans the waiting rooms. Pushes a broom all day.'

'So what's not to like?' The boy moves closer to the counter. He can see a rack of girlie magazines tucked tight against the wall. Hair wax and condoms.

The man shrugs. 'It was twenty years ago. My uncle was my hero. He had flown on a great silver bird and landed right next to His Majesty. When my father told me we were going all the way to see Uncle Stan – to tell him his sister had died – I thought I'd died with her and gone straight up to heaven. London! When I arrived, I burst into tears. The sky was full of rainclouds and when you breathed, that grey London air tasted bad. My uncle had changed. Stan the Man was now a tired shrunken piece of nothing in particular. He'd been a sharp dresser. Once had his picture in the *Gleaner*! Now his poor man's clothes fell from him in unwashed shiny creases. He lived in a room. One small room with everything in it! Grey squawking birds were perched across his window ledge. You could not move an inch without stepping over his laundry, or his little metal fire, or his poor excuse of a kitchen. Kitchen! My mother refused to eat. For three weeks she ate nothing but apples. My uncle was living off canned tomato soup and the pepper pot.'

'The trains don't pay? Is that what you're saying?'

'No. That's the least of it, man. Oh, it wasn't just my uncle. He told us, don't look down your noses, this is how everyone lives in London. But I didn't believe him. Walking from the station, being glared at, spat at and gollywogged, I'd seen all the big tall houses with their fancy lights glowing. The ladies wrapped in fur like film stars. He wasn't telling me those nose-in-the-air, shoo-boy-shoo ladies sat on a lemonade crate eating canned soup, elbows bumping the wallpaper, their dainty feet resting on a piece of scorched rug. What he meant was, this is how *Jamaicans* live in London.'

'Where in London?' asks the boy, looking nervous.

'Seven Sisters.'

'Sounds nice.'

The man leans over the counter. The boy can see a teardrop of pepper sauce hanging on his shirt. 'Well, I'll tell you something man, them London's Seven Sisters have nothing to do with the stars.'

'Did you see Brixton?'

'Brixton!' He laughs. '*Cha!* Brixton is wall-to-wall Jamaicans, and you know what that means?'

'It's like home?' says the boy.

'It's like my uncle's shitty train life. Only bigger.'

'Twenty years,' the boy reminds him. 'That's a long time ago. The English still had their flags flying on our poles. I was two years old and crying for a drum kit.'

'You are wrong,' says the man, clicking his bony fingers. 'For the immigrant, twenty years is *nothing*.'


The water cracks like a horse whip. When Noël opens his eyes the light appears in small criss-cross bars. He can feel the lilo swaying, and for a few long seconds he thinks he might have left the confines of his swimming pool and drifted out to sea.

'Boss?' he hears. 'Are you okay, Boss?'

He feels a wet hand next to his ear, then his straw hat flips away, revealing a dazzling curtain of sunlight. Patrice is panting. 'Boss?' he's saying. 'Have you been out here all morning, Boss?'

Noël wants to answer but his lips appear to be glued. He turns to see Patrice treading water. His shirtsleeves are billowing. He's pulling Noël and the lilo towards the steps, blowing water from his mouth, like a whale.

Waterlogged, Patrice manages to manoeuvre Noël into the nearest wicker chair where he sits slumped, his body a half-hearted fountain splashing onto the stones.

'Mad dogs,' he manages. 'Mad dogs.'

Patrice is squeezing out his own shirtsleeves, the water dripping from his face, as his eyes move towards the table, where the remains of Noël's uneaten sandwich sit curling on the plate.

'You ate nothing, Boss?'

'I think I had a biscuit.'

'You want a glass of water now?'

'I think I'm wet enough.'

Patrice sloshes towards the table and retrieves Noël's cigarettes and his lighter. 'You could have drowned, Boss,' he says, lighting two cigarettes.

'I wasn't drowning, I was floating,' says Noël, 'and if truth be known, I found it very relaxing.'

'Heatstroke, Boss. You can die of it.'

'I can think of worse fucking ways to go.'

They sit side by side in their ever-widening puddles. Noël starts singing, *'Just walking in the rain, getting soaking wet . . .'* When he forgets the words, he whistles. 'He was almost stone deaf you know.'

'Who?'

'Johnnie Ray. 'The Nabob of Sob'.'

'Never heard of him,' says Patrice. 'And what's nabob?'

'Someone powerful. He came here. To Firefly. Drank us out of house and home but he was very charming with it. Very sweet. Yes, for all his problems, he was a very sweet boy.'

'Famous people tend to drink a lot, Boss,' says Patrice. 'I've noticed that.'

'You have? Well I don't, not really. It's a terrible weakness. Of course, I drank a lot less when I was younger, I needed to keep on the ball, you can't work like I did and get half-cut every night.'

Patrice shakes out his feet. His toes are already covered in dust.

Noël looks up. 'What happened to your T-shirt?'

'My T-shirt, Boss?'

'You were wearing a white T-shirt in Kingston. In the book shop.'

Patrice laughs. 'The heatstroke has arrived, Boss. You'd better go inside. Lie down. I don't want Mr Payn throwing me out before I've heard back from the Ritz.'

'You really weren't in Kingston?' Noël puzzles. 'Shit.'

'Oh, I was in Kingston all right, Boss, but I wasn't in a book shop, I was with my cousin Joe. I had to give him the letter, you know, my letter for the Ritz.'

'You left me all morning for that!' says Noël. 'Christ! Have you never heard of fucking stamps?'

At five o'clock, Patrice calls the doctor. Noël is in bed. He looks flushed. He's been complaining of a headache, saying that he feels very cold. His usual doctor is unavailable. An Englishman called Reeve arrives, driving a polished black Daimler. Patrice can't help but walk around the car, admiring it.

'I had it shipped over,' says Reeve as he opens the driver's door. 'What do you think? Kid leather seats. Walnut dash. Everything top notch. Does your master have one of these in his garage? I suppose he might have a fleet of them.'

'No, sir. Not in Jamaica.'

'Don't blame him,' says the doctor, looking towards the house and pulling off his driving gloves. 'Not with these roads. Mind you, he doesn't have to live here all year. I've been here since '55. I have to have some recompense. I have to have a little bit of comfort in my life.'

Reeve is a small man with thinning brown hair. His shoes have Cuban heels and he walks slightly on tiptoe as if trying to squeeze out his height.

Patrice leads the way to the house. He had tried calling Mr Payn, but the line was engaged. When Noël had heard about it he'd thrown his espadrille at the wall. It had hit the side of a picture. 'Don't go blabbing to Mr Payn. It's only fucking sunstroke. He'll think I'm a doddering fool. Again.'

The doctor pauses in the kitchen. 'I'd like to wash my hands,' he says, looking around the room. 'It's very small. I'd no idea it was quite this compact.'

Patrice moves a few dirty glasses from the bowl. A

111

half-eaten mango. 'It's his retreat,' he says. 'It's where he likes to work. To get away from it all.'

'Oh, I've heard about the parties at Blue Harbour,' says the doctor, running the tap. 'I've never been invited. They sound like great fun.'

'Yes, sir,' says Patrice, handing the doctor a towel. 'All the famous people. All the great and the good of the island.'

Reeve gives a high, false laugh. 'No chance for me there, then,' he screeches. 'I'm only a doctor!'

At the bottom of the stairs Patrice hesitates. 'He always puts on a brave face,' he says. 'I think the sun has affected his mind. He thought he saw me in Kingston this morning, but he's been at the house all day.'

'Perhaps he nodded off?' says the doctor.

'He sleeps a lot, but I don't know, sir. Sometimes he sways. He can barely stand upright. He forgets things.'

'I'm the same,' says Reeve. 'I left my wallet at the Upton. I didn't worry too much. They're very honest. They called me that night. Everything in its place. I knew I could trust them. Now, direct me to the patient.'

'Yes, but all the sleeping and forgetting?'

'It's that sort of climate. Come on, quick smart, I haven't got all day.'

112

Noël hears them on the stairs. The sharp clip-clop of the doctor's heels, the slower, softer tramp of Patrice. He quickly wriggles himself into a straighter position. He looks at his bedside cabinet. He hides a broken biscuit. A filthy-looking tissue.

'Well, well, well.' The doctor comes breezing into the room, holding out his hand. 'This is a pleasure. Peter Reeve. Formerly of London. Now resident in Jamaica.'

Noël grins. His false teeth are chafing. He thinks he might have blisters. He wishes he could take them out and let his gums relax. 'Where are you from originally?' Noël asks. 'I don't believe it's London.'

The doctor looks pained. 'I had an office in Harley Street,' he says. 'For a little while.'

'But you were born in . . . ?'

'Hartlepool.'

Noël says nothing as Patrice backs out of the room, saying he'll return with the refreshments. 'Tea?' he asks.

'Oh,' says the doctor, poking a finger down his collar, 'anything but that.'

Standing at the bedside, the doctor appears to be examining the room. He moves towards the window. 'What a view,' he says. 'Magnificent.'

'It's probably the sun,' says Noël. His face feels tight; like he's wearing a mask that has shrunk.

The doctor looks puzzled. 'No, it really is beautiful.'

'I was talking about my ailment.'

'Ah,' he says. 'I see.'

From his bag he produces a thermometer. 'Put it under your tongue.'

While Noël sits inconvenienced, the doctor chats. 'We all have a little too much sun now and then. Stands to reason. The tourists of course are terrible. Skin like milk and they lie like herrings expecting to be golden by teatime. We have your LP records,' he says. 'They remind us of home.'

Noël has a vision of Hartlepool. Flat caps. Grey docks. A college. He can see the doctor's home life in Jamaica – a gregarious wife who's a little too fond of the Dubonnet, two children with dazzling white knee socks and weekly elocution lessons, all traces of Jamaica ironed out, with a box of Robin's starch and rich Yorkshire pudding.

'It's a little high.' The doctor frowns, examining the tube. 'But not excessively so. Are you in pain?'

'A headache.'

'We saw *Blithe Spirit*,' he says. 'An amateur production but they could have been professionals. They were as good as anything I'd seen in Kingston, or in London for that matter. Perhaps we could say they were better than professionals?'

114

'We could?' says Noël, wincing with the pain stabbing through his head. 'How?'

The doctor smiles. 'Well, they have day jobs of course. They have less time to learn their lines and practise. And the costumes were lovely.'

Noël squeezes his fingernails into the palms of his hands. 'I'm sure they were very entertaining.'

'So you've a headache? Bit of a tingle on the skin, eh? Some good old-fashioned cold cream should do the trick. And an aspirin. Drink plenty of water.'

'Is that it?'

'Of course, you should stay out of the sun for a while, but that goes without saying. How are you otherwise? Fit and well?'

Noël swallows. 'I've been walking,' he says. 'My doctor recommended it.'

'Excellent. And I see you have a swimming pool.'

'I think I might have slept on the airbed.'

'Like I said, it happens.' Reeve dips into his pocket for a pack of cigarettes. 'Menthol,' he says, offering one to Noël. 'You'll find them very smooth on the lungs.'

'Drink, sir?' asks Patrice. The doctor looks at the tray, the jug of iced water, the bottles of Coca-Cola, the bowl of sliced lime. He consults his watch. 'It's almost six,' he says. 'Do you happen to have gin? Pink gin?'

Noël raises his eyebrows. It makes his forehead sting. 'Gin for the doctor,' he says. 'I'll have water. For now. And could you find me the aspirin? I think I need four.'

'Four, Boss? You're supposed to take two.'

'Four won't kill him,' says Reeve. 'I saw a woman last week in Ocho Rios. She'd taken twenty. She was still alive and kicking when I left her.'

The doctor takes his gin and stands by the window. 'I've treated others like you, you know. Other famous people.'

'Really?'

'I saw Terry Thomas. He was here on holiday. He had a terrible throat. And I almost met Cliff Richard, but someone got there before me.'

'Who?' says Noël. 'God?'

'Oh he isn't dead,' says Reeve. 'Is he?'

The room feels small. Noël wonders if his forehead is actually moving, there's such a pounding pain behind it. When he touches the skin, he can feel something pulsing on his fingertips. A heartbeat.

'And now I have you.' The doctor turns towards Noël and grins. 'I was wondering if perhaps I might use your name in my brochure? For my private practice. Nothing too vulgar. Just your name would do. Perhaps a small picture?'

'I don't think so.'

'But you have done advertisements,' he says. 'I've seen them on the billboards.'

Noël takes a sip of his water. 'Well, if you're offering me that kind of money, how on earth could I possibly refuse?'

The doctor looks flustered. 'Well, I . . . Well, I . . .'

'Look,' says Noël, 'could you go now? I'm really rather tired.'

Reeve drains the last few drops of his gin. He sets the dirty glass on the windowsill. The remaining cubes of ice make a popping sound.


1927. A cabin. The *President Pierce*. Sailing to Hong Kong. Noël feels every roll of the ocean, every squall and swell. The corridor rattles with unsettled porters' trolleys, the groans of the sick, the laughter of the cabin boys who are all very young, full of bravado and used to it.

There are terrible smells of vomit, antiseptic, stale fried food. With a bucket at his side, Noël tries to focus on something solid. He sees the ceiling as a square blank canvas. Pictures appear, silent and flickering, like a visit to the Rialto before the talkies came. Jack's here, waving. *It's all right*, Noël wants to tell him. *You can stop now, we're sailing.* Jack's wearing Noël's fur coat. There's a band. He can hear it. A man with a large handlebar moustache is playing the tuba.

117

Drums. The swinging trombones seem to be rammed so close to his face, Noël can't help himself flinching.

And now he sees himself on stage. He's a member of the audience, sitting in the front row of the stalls. Such expensive tickets. He's looking at a vision of himself in costume and greasepaint, playing the part of Lewis Dodd in *The Constant Nymph*. He snaps quite suddenly in the middle of the performance. His knees have gone to jelly. He can see that. He cries his way through it. *So this is how I looked?* The audience are whispering. A man on his right says, *Bloody awful show*.

Honolulu appears at the windows before the ship comes juddering into the busy harbour. The portholes are crammed with girls in grass skirts, undulating their hips, their necks garlanded with *leis*, playing ukuleles, slide guitars and the tremoloa. Noël rolls towards the corner of his cabin. He tucks himself between the waste-paper basket (ballasted to the floor with a large brass screw) and a heavy 'easy' chair. Perhaps they won't see him in the corner? It's a very dark corner.

A doctor wearing a jaunty sailor's cap and attended by a group of dancing nurses throws Noël a bottle of pills.

'What are they?' he asks, the bottle jumping like a red-hot coal from his hands.

'A sedative,' says the doctor. 'A knock-out. You really need to take them.'

'Or else?'

The nurses look alarmed. They stop their rhythmical wriggling. They push their little fingers into their blushing powdered cheeks.

'You might lose your genius,' the doctor says, producing a ukulele from his pocket and strumming a few hairy notes. 'Or you might go mad and lose everything.'

The ship rams into the side of the dock. The ceiling peels back, revealing a square piece of sky, a breeze moves over his face, it whistles through his ears and makes him think of a kettle.


'At least the room's stopped moving,' says Noël. 'I appear to have acquired my sea legs.'

Patrice is holding a bowl of chicken soup. 'My mother made it,' he says, perching on the bed. 'It cured my sister's whooping cough.'

'Then I'd better give it a try.'

Patrice holds the spoon, and for a second Noël thinks Patrice might dip it into the bowl to feed him, but now it's in Noël's hand, the handle is warm, and the soup tastes like an old-fashioned Sunday, with extra spice and pepper.

'Did that dim-witted quack leave Miguel the bill?' Noël asks.

'No, Boss. He gave the bill to me. Should I take it to Blue Harbour in the morning?'

Noël shakes his head. 'Leave it here. Don't say a word, not one bloody word. I'll pay it.'

Patrice moves around the room. He puts the sandals and espadrilles into pairs. He opens a new jar of cold cream. 'You need more on your forehead,' he says.

'Fucking doctor. Fucking charlatan,' he says. 'Cold cream and aspirin? Nurse Dot in the *Gleaner* could have told me that. It's bloody common sense. Don't tell me how much he charged. I don't want to end this shitting day with a fucking heart attack.'

'You should have seen his car,' says Patrice.

Noël grunts. 'Should I?'

'A Daimler, Boss.'

'Show-off. Only a man from Hartlepool would want to drive a Daimler in the fucking West Indies. Harley Street my arse.'

Noël finishes the soup. 'Do give your mother my very best regards,' he says, dabbing his lips with a tissue. 'The soup was simply delicious.'

'She'll be thrilled, Boss. She's famous for her soup.'

'She should can it.'

'How's the headache?'

'Passing.'

Noël looks at the window. The world is too bright. He has no idea what time it is. His head feels foggy and his tongue feels enormous. And why is he lying in bed? Isn't it too early for bed? His face is tight. The cold cream makes everything sticky.

'You don't have to hang about here,' he tells Patrice. 'Go and do something useful.'

'You've been sleeping for a while, Boss.'

'So?'

'Mr Cole brought a box of groceries. He came and had a look at you.'

'Shit.'

'I told him you had a very slight hangover. That you were sleeping it off.'

'Good thinking.'

'Do you need anything, Boss?'

Noël purses his lips. 'Well, now . . . I wouldn't mind having a go on the back of Steve McQueen's motorbike, but as I'm quite incapacitated I think I'll stick with my book.'

'I'll come back in half an hour, Boss. If I see Mr McQueen hanging about the yard, I'll tell him that you're busy. I'm sure he'll be very disappointed.'

'If he's wearing his leathers send him straight up. I'm weak, but I think I could manage it.'

# 6

Boys. There had always been boys. His mother had sent generous invitations on little white cards. They usually came. The playmates sitting cross-legged in their sailor suits watched the little girl dancing on the rug, hair curled, a frilly skirt wafting at her rather chubby knees. They'd clapped their sticky hands and giggled when she'd curtsied. They'd splashed raspberry cordial down their matelot jackets, much to the annoyance of their nannies, or their mothers, who told the boys to say thank you to that nice Noël Coward for keeping them all amused. The boys looked puzzled but they shook his small pale hand and thanked him just the same.

Next came the self-assured theatricals. Wet eyes. Reedy voices. A rudimentary swagger. Boys called Charles who wriggled their undersized shoulders and with a slight toss of their heads called themselves Cha-cha, Carlotta, or Little Miss Charlene. Boys who might place a hand on your knee, because they'd seen the leading man do the same. Mind you, they were only copying, it wasn't really their predilection – though the boy with the rosebud lips and smooth black hair knew exactly what he was doing. He'd even charged a penny for it.

The boys suddenly grew taller. Wider. They had scrubbed pink necks which they splashed with their sister's cologne (Devon Violets was always very popular). They winked. Noël found them all teeth-gratingly irritating. These were the hangers-on. Usually insipid. They had limp flapping hands. They moved around in clusters, heads together, screeching away like girls.

Men had a confidence. They'd had years of experience. They wore expensive clothes with hand-stitched labels – Noël particularly noticed the labels, the sight of which had provoked him into a little light theft from the likes of Anderson & Sheppard, who sold such beautiful clothes. Or Selfridges. Nothing too big mind you – just a few pairs of socks, or a hankie.

These sophisticated men drove motor cars. They slapped their calfskin wallets onto counters. They knew how to order in restaurants. Read French. Manage a few words of Spanish with the syrup-eyed waiter. When they lit cigarettes their fingers were dancing. Their lips tasted of cognac, engine oil, and dark cigarillos. Inside their Harris tweed jackets the linings were silk. Like water. Their shoulders were muscular. Bulky. They explored the body thoroughly, and without any fumbling apologies. When they kissed, their bristles had made goose bumps spring along the soft insides of his newly downed thighs.

Now in sleep they're back again. He has no control. They're here behind his eyes and their fresh unchanged faces make his stomach ache. The artist. The dancer. The New Zealander who'd kept him sane in hospital during the First World War. His nerves again. Geoffrey played the piano. He'd shown Noël his place of escape – a gap in the outside wall. They'd run all the way into town, laughing. They were lucky they didn't get caught.

He can see actors he'd had flings with. They'd kept snapshots of their women in their worn leather pocketbooks. They'd had ploughed perfect hair. Crisp white teeth. They couldn't pass a mirror without stopping for at least twenty seconds. Their lies sounded like poetry. Of course there were other kinds. Rough kinds. A man in the building trade showed him a secret tattoo. A barber sucked him off in a room at the back of his shop as they heard the doorbell chiming with new customers. An English prince. A surgeon once took him to bed. Cradled him. Noël was agonisingly smitten. He'd waited for the telephone to ring. A letter. There was a surge of disappointment. Vomiting. Anger. He really could have kicked himself. Again.

When he wakes he feels bruised. He's exhausted and impotent. The dreams keep coming. Perhaps it's the pills?

He sits in a shade so dense he can feel himself shivering. Patrice pours him a glass of lemonade. 'Are you feeling any better today, Boss?'

'Yes,' says Noël, pressing at his temple. 'I really think I am.'

'What about tomorrow?'

'Tomorrow?' asks Noël.

'You said Mr Payn and Mr Cole would be coming up to dinner on Sunday. That I could practise silver service for the Ritz.'

'It's Sunday tomorrow? Really?'

'Yes, Boss.'

'No.' Noël shakes his head. 'I can't believe that it's Sunday tomorrow.'

'I've been reading *Festive Food*, Boss. I was thinking about salmon.'

'You're not going as a chef,' Noël tells him. 'I wouldn't

worry too much about the food. Mr Payn and Mr Cole will eat anything.'

'Would you like their heads leaving on? Only, in the picture they put red grapes where their eyes should have been.'

'Whatever you think best.'

'I have no red grapes, Boss. Only black. Do you think they'll be having salmon today? There are day guests at Blue Harbour.'

Noël sips his lemonade. 'No,' he sighs. 'It'll probably be chicken.'

When he takes himself inside he sees Gertrude Lawrence sitting with her feet up on the sofa. 'I know you're dead,' he says. 'You're not in *Blithe* fucking *Spirit*. You never would have made it as Elvira, the critics would have crucified you.'

She lifts her nose in the air. Noël feels like weeping. 'You look beautiful,' he says. 'Dead or otherwise. I'll give you that. Or perhaps it's the ether?'

Gertrude looks put out, but she says nothing. Noël fumbles through his record collection. He finds a scratchy recording of 'Has Anybody Seen Our Ship?'. As it moves around the turntable he mouths the words and Gert does the same. A vaporous double act.

He sits holding a cushion. He looks at the light streaming through the window, the way it catches the pillars of dust. Of course Gert will vanish in a minute, she'll melt into nothing, again.

He was at the races when he heard that she'd died. Sitting with his cushion he can't quite think of the year, his mind has lost all its calendars, but it was the fifties and Gert was far too young. His friends had been appalled at his grief. They'd sneered at his weeping. Was Noël play-acting? What a drama queen! He hadn't seen Gertrude for ages. He was always slagging her off. So why all these tears?

The record spins silently. It crackles. He moves to find another one, throwing the cushion at the space that was Gert. He wavers over 'Someday I'll Find You'. 'Are you kidding? If I play this I'll be certifiable. It isn't about you anyway. Listen. Why the fuck would I sing about a woman?'

He chooses the soundtrack to *Carousel*. Rodgers and Hammerstein always know how to cheer him up. He holds no grudges regarding popularity or box-office receipts. They deserve their recognition. *This Was a Real Nice Clam Bake*.

Without too much effort he can see everything on stage. The women in their pretty, old-fashioned dresses, swaying in time to the music. The shimmering carousel. He can lose himself in it. The world slows down. The hour, the day of the week, the year, will mean nothing as the music fills the room. He'll see

127

all the coloured lights. The dancing. *You'll Never Walk Alone*.

'Are the house-guests famous, Mr Coward?'

Noël looks around. My God! Gertrude isn't really here. Is she? 'House-guests? What house-guests?' he shivers. 'Where?'

Noël's back on the terrace. Patrice has been watering the flower pots with his shirtsleeves pushed to his elbows. His trousers are rolled to his shins.

'At Blue Harbour, Boss.'

'Oh,' he says, relieved. 'I've really no idea.'

'Famous people like Blue Harbour. I've seen them, Boss. I've seen them arriving as film stars and thirty minutes later they're paddling like children.'

'You'll miss all that in London.'

'Oh no, Boss. The Ritz is full of famous people. Even the Beatles have stayed at the Ritz.'

*'Yeah, yeah, yeah.'*

'And after working at Blue Harbour I will take it all in my stride.'

Noël reaches for his cigarettes. He can see the water shining on Patrice's jutting ankle bone. 'I think you will find that the so-called stars in London are a little more fucking uptight and they don't go in for small talk, especially with their waiter, or their new Jamaican pot boy.'

128

'They might remember me, Boss. They might want to relive their warm Blue Harbour memories.'

Noël shakes his head. 'The Ritz is full of stuck-up snobby cunts, so I doubt it.'

'I remember when that man was here, that film-star actor who played at splashing on the lilo with a teacloth on his head.'

'Sir Alec Guinness.'

'Yes, that's him. I was helping Mr Foster in the garden, and Mr Guinness, he made himself a most exotic costume out of the cut bougainvilleas, and he told me to call him Alice, oh we did laugh at that, and his wife was very charming, and we all played along, until the blooms began to wilt.'

'Let me offer some advice.'

'Yes, Boss?'

'If you ever have the good fortune of seeing Sir Alec's face hovering over a soup bowl, a prawn cocktail, or a plate of Ritz crackers, keep your mouth shut and don't mention the cross-dressing.'

'Discreet and invisible, Boss.'

'Perhaps you'd like a little rehearsal?'


His head feels tender. There's a tingling across his face like the aftermath of a large electric shock. His hands are the colour of freshly boiled lobsters. The world is too noisy. Lying on a sunbed in the shade he stuffs his ears with tissues. The birds are annoying him. The crickets are too loud. The tree frogs. Everything.

'Patrice!' he shouts, wincing at his voice. 'Patrice!'

It takes a while for Patrice to appear.

'I'm sorry,' he says. 'I was thinking about the salmon. Yes, Boss?'

'I could hear you,' says Noël. 'You weren't fucking thinking, you were singing. Now, what was that song?'

'Song, Boss?'

'On the radio. On the very loud radio. It sounded so very fucking jolly.'

'Jolly?' Patrice tightens his eyebrows. Smiles. Then he starts to sing. '*Get up in the morning, slaving for bread, sir . . .*'

'Patrice,' says Noël, holding up his hand. 'Could you possibly bring the radio out to me?'

'Yes, Boss.' He grins, doing his version of the twist. 'Pool party!'

Noël attempts to rise. When Patrice returns holding the Grundig like a pet, the radio is full of a man selling beer nuts. 'You want it tuning, Boss?' he says. 'They play calypso around twelve o'clock.'

'I'm not fond of calypso,' says Noël, heaving himself off the sunbed and tottering towards the edge of the veranda. 'Calypso reminds me of those very bad TV commercials for reconstituted rum-flavoured

130

puddings.' He holds out his hand. 'I'll take it,' he says. 'I'll do the tuning.'

He lets the radio drop over the balustrade where it smashes onto the concrete. Patrice puts his hand to his mouth, but says nothing.

'Now,' says Noël. 'Perhaps you might go down and retrieve the batteries? Mr Payn only bought them the other day. They might come in handy for a torch.'

'Yes, Boss.'

'No need to look quite so morose,' Noël tells him. 'Nothing died here.'

He watches Patrice as he walks with a curious grace towards the broken radio. He collects the pieces as if they were small shattered bones.

Noël settles his grilled red hands. He thinks of the boys from his earlier dream, and though they had unsettled him for an hour or two, he would like to bring them back. On his own terms. No whimsical tots in sailor suits. No Cha-Cha Charlies. He would like to dream about his (sadly, former) sex life.

He pictures nude young men glistening with oil. Rooms appear with tasselled silk cushions thrown across the floor, towers of fruit, small turquoise pools. Gold. A debauched sultan's palace. He watches a plump Arab boy. A curly-headed blond. The Greek-type. He watches Graham going at it hammer and

131

tongs with someone else. A stranger. A groaner. But you can't plan your dreams and the men evaporate into the darkness. They shrug their shoulders and throw him a wave as they close the door firmly behind them.

An unfamiliar theatre. There are no backdrops, no curtains, no plush velvet seats. There's nothing resembling an orchestra pit. Noël stands to one side in what might just pass as an auditorium – there are rows of plastic bucket chairs – but the room looks like part of a factory. Red bricks and dull grey paint. Duct tape on the carpet.

A girl walks past him. She's wearing jeans, a green gingham shirt and squeaky canvas shoes. Her hair has been pulled into a childish-looking ponytail. Her wrists are hidden by a cache of Indian bracelets. When she reaches the stage she thrusts two fingers into her mouth and whistles. 'Bruce!' she shouts. 'Are you back there? Bruce!'

A man comes lumbering onto the stage. He looks like a motor mechanic. He pushes a hand through his mop of greasy hair. 'For God's sake, what's with all the shouting?'

'Noël Coward's here,' the girl tells him. Then she lowers her voice. '*He's waiting.*'

Bruce fiddles around in his pocket and produces a crushed cigarette. 'Bugger,' he says. 'It's my last, it'll have to do. Noël Coward's here already? I mean, who the hell is he anyway?'

The girl laughs. Noël can see her ponytail bouncing up and down. 'He's famous,' she says. 'Or he used to be. He wrote all those awful stuffy plays about the aristocracy. You know, they had butlers, wore silk dressing gowns, they puffed their fags through long cigarette holders and' (she affects a high snooty voice) *'Could somebody pass me a cocktail?'*

'Hello, grandad,' says Bruce, looking over the girl's narrow shoulder. 'We have your script in the green room.'

Noël follows Bruce. He can see patches on his jeans. Mud flecks on the hems. His shirt appears to be fastened wrong. When they get to the green room, it's nothing but a few ugly chairs, a table with a jar of instant coffee and a chipped brown teapot. There is an electric ring for a saucepan. A smell of something scorched. On the wall a crumpled poster for a production of a play called *Bastard* hangs from strips of yellow Sellotape. 'I was in that,' says Bruce. 'I was the bastard.'

'Is it well known?' asks Noël, moving a little closer and narrowing his eyes. 'Who's the playwright?'

Bruce laughs. 'Playwright? There isn't a playwright. And of course it's well known. Really. Isn't everyone acquainted with a bastard?'

133

A script is thrown at him. It's very flimsy. There are less than ten pages. *'Is this it?'*

'Well of course it isn't the whole play,' the girl tells him with a shrug. 'It's just the bare bones. We make the rest of it up. On the night. We improvise.'

Noël shakes his head. 'Well, it's not for me, thank you.'

He feels a heavy hand on his shoulder. 'You signed the contract,' says Bruce. 'If you don't go on, we'll sue you.'

The girl hands him a cup of coffee. There are small yellow blobs floating on the surface. 'We've run out of sugar,' she tells him. 'And don't worry about the milk. It's powdered. It doesn't go off.'

He sits and reads his eight and a half lines. He plays a character called Hoop. 'What kind of name is Hoop?' he asks.

Bruce crouches in front of him. 'It's a name that represents his life,' he says, illustrating the concept with his hands. 'A circle. The way he jumps through hoops. We did wonder if it might be short for Hooper. It could be. And of course there's the hollow in the centre of a hoop. A nothing. Hoop always feels like he's nothing.'

A costume rail appears. A woman dressed like a gypsy throws him a thin brown suit. 'If it doesn't fit, I could always take it in,' she tells him. 'But we only have an hour.'

'An hour?' says Noël. 'We haven't had a read-through, never mind rehearsed.'

'Rehearsals kill the play,' says the girl. 'The audience want something breathing. Something that's alive.'

When he next looks down he's wearing the suit. The hems of the trousers almost cover his shoes. 'I look shambolic,' he says. 'Am I playing the part of a tramp?'

'I wore that suit in *Hamlet*,' Bruce tells him.

'Hamlet wore a cheap brown suit?' Noël doesn't know what's more incredible: Hamlet wearing the suit, or the company doing a play – with a script.

'In our version,' Bruce tells him, 'Hamlet wasn't the prince of Denmark. He was the crown prince of Dulwich.'

'Dulwich has a prince?'

'It has a car showroom. Hamlet was the manager.'

Noël tries to button the jacket. It feels a little tight. When he puts his hands inside the pockets he finds a book of matches and a fossilised sausage roll.

'So that's where it went,' says Bruce.

At the side of the stage Noël can see the play in motion. The first few rows of the audience are a cheap-looking crowd. A man has his bare arms folded. A girl is chewing gum. He feels sick. What's his first line again? He looks at the script. There are pages missing. It's thinner than it used to be. Three pages.

'I left it on the bus.' That's his first line. When does he say it? On stage a girl is hanging washing. She's pegging a pair of knickers when he feels a nudge in his ribs to go on.

'I left it on the bus,' he says. The pale lights swallow him. The audience start to laugh. Are they laughing at his trousers? He can hardly walk in them without tripping. He feels like a clown.

The girl stops pegging. 'Oh, Hoop,' she says. 'What'll I tell my husband? He won't believe me. He'll think I've spent it again. What are you going to do?'

Noël pulls at his collar. He can feel the cold burning eyes of the audience. He opens his mouth. Surely his next line doesn't fit? According to the script he's supposed to say, 'I only met Albert once. He had a dog with him.' His mouth remains open. The audience are whispering. Tittering. Someone coughs loudly.

'I could always ring the bus depot,' he says. The theatre is in uproar. What's so funny? Isn't he supposed to improvise? The girl looks puzzled. From the side of the stage a voice hisses, '*I only met Albert once.*' Noël can't move. The prompt repeats his line. His legs are like lead. The lights are too stark, too intense. He stumbles. He can feel himself falling. He hears a menacing slow hand clap. The air rushing past him. Then nothing.

\*   \*   \*

'I need something to keep me awake,' he tells Coley. 'I'm always asleep. Always dreaming.'

'Sleep's good for you. It's healing. As long as it's not in the sun . . .'

'Healing?' Noël hisses and narrows his eyes. 'If it's healing, I should be fitter than a twelve-year-old. I should be doing fucking cartwheels.'

Coley looks uncomfortable. He pulls at a loose piece of thread on his trousers. 'If you were a little more active,' he starts, 'had a little more company, then perhaps you wouldn't sleep so much during the day.'

Noël slams down his coffee cup, losing half its contents over *The Railway Children*. 'Active! I haven't come here to be active,' he snarls. 'Hell! I'm here because I want to do nothing! At my age, and after all my hard work, I deserve to do nothing!'

'Talking,' Coley swallows. 'That's all I meant. A good conversation might help keep you more alert, more awake.'

Noël screams. 'Talking? I'm sick of talking. Talking wears me out. I like silence. I like solitary confinement. Perhaps I should apply to fucking Wormwood Scrubs?' As soon as the words are out of his mouth he thinks, *The Scrubs wouldn't take me, I'm not allowed in England, I've used up all my time.*

'I'm only trying to help.' Coley stands up. He beckons

137

Patrice. 'You'd better get a cloth,' he says, pointing to the spillage.

'He's a useless cunt,' says Noël. 'Not to mention fucking annoying.'

'Miguel will be back on Monday, first thing. Patrice won't bother you then.'

'Hallelujah. He gets on my nerves. And he's too bloody noisy. If he isn't whistling he's jabbering on about nothing. About the bloody Ritz.'

Patrice wipes the mess. He picks up the book. 'I'll try to rescue it, Boss.'

'Don't worry too much. I know how it ends.'

'He tries,' says Coley, as Patrice slinks inside with the wet book and the cloth. 'He just wants to be a waiter.'

'In England?'

'He's heard about the Ritz. He's just looking for adventure.'

'Then he'll be disappointed,' says Noël. 'Because the Ritz will be looking for slaves.'

# 7

S UNDAY. PATRICE stands at the table, polishing the silver, talking about his mother who will be wending her way towards church, wearing her best polka-dot dress and her large netted hat, praying for the souls of her family, who have badly let her down. Uncles, well past their prime, who have taken young girls as brides. Her ugly drug-addict niece. A wayward sister in Montego Bay who has four children with four different men, and who has trouble remembering which child belongs to which absent father. *Ach, she'll say, with her hands on her hips. They don't come visiting me none, so what does it matter, cha?* Patrice has done a perfect imitation of his mother imitating her youngest sister, Bernice. Even Noël glances up from his paper and smiles.

'Do you go to church, Boss?' asks Patrice, setting down a knife. 'I've never seen you going to church.'

'I don't do church,' says Noël. 'Not if I can help it.'

'As a boy I did an awful lot of praying,' says Patrice. 'I knelt so long and hard I had sores across my knees.'

'How Catholic. And were your prayers ever answered?'

'No, Boss. I never got me a microphone on a stand or a red scooter with flags on the handlebars. In fact, I got nothing very much for all my hard work praying, and though my mother told me not to bother God asking for possessions, I always did say, if you don't ask nothing, you don't get nothing.'

'I thought you wanted a drum kit,' says Noël.

'Drums? I never wanted drums.'

Noël sits with his feet on a stool, circling his ankles. He's read that this simple exercise is very good for the heart. It gets the blood moving. He reaches for his glasses. Looks at the crossword. Is the print getting smaller?

'Church, or no church,' says Patrice, 'Sunday is a good day for relaxing.'

'Amen to that,' says Noël.

He's been awake since 6.45, with no recollection of his dreams. He's eaten grapefruit salad. A small poached egg. He's walked around the swimming pool. Twice.

'Do what one is told,' says Noël.

'Yes, Boss. After polishing the silver, I'm taking out the washing.'

'Six down,' says Noël, sucking the end of his biro. *'Obey.'*

Patrice spends most of the day in the kitchen. He's never looked happier. He wears an apron with the words 'Hot Stuff' embroidered on the bib. It's stained with tomato sauce, grease and streaks of turmeric. When he presents Noël with his chicken salad lunch the radishes look like budding roses and the tomatoes have been cut with fancy jagged lines.

'Very impressive,' says Noël, reaching for the salad cream.

'Waiters have to take an interest in the food, Boss,' he says. 'I've been reading all about it.'

Noël lifts his ragged eyebrows.

'You see, Boss, a customer might want some advice. He might wonder what's in the mixed grill. Does it include kidney or pork sausage? Is the soup spicy? He might be asking what makes up the sauce, the pie, or the mushroom risotto.'

'Mushrooms, I presume. Are their diners particularly stupid?' Noël glances at the curling yellow label before tipping the salad cream bottle and slapping its sticky glass bottom. A glug of pale goo lands neatly by the

141

lettuce. 'Do you read French?' he asks, now being very liberal with the salt.

Patrice shakes his head. He pushes his hands into the kangaroo pocket of his apron. 'Why?'

'Most of the menus in such highfalutin establishments are written in French,' Noël tells him. '*Terrine Rustique, Coquilles St Jacques, Salade Verte, Poisson du Jour, Escargots, Baba au Rhum . . .*'

'Even in London, Boss?'

'Especially in London and especially at the Ritz.'

'French.'

'Oh, don't look so worried,' says Noël, spearing a flowery radish. 'It's only food. You can learn the basics. I'll get Coley to write you a list. You can take it on the banana boat. It'll help pass the time.'

'Thank you, Boss.'

'Think nothing of it. Now, you could be a dear and fetch me *le pain et le beurre*?'

'Boss?'

'Bread and butter.'

'Coming right up, Boss. *Le pain et le beurre.*'

Noël smiles. 'Thank you, Patrice. *Merci.*'

After lunch he dozes. He stretches across the bed and he tells himself this is what people do on Sundays. Especially at his age. People all over England will be sluggish, full of roast beef, they'll have finished off the remains of Auntie May's sherry trifle, the dirty plates will be stacked by their sinks, and now they'll have their feet up, listening to the wireless, or the television. Their rooms will be humming with a very old film. Cowboys and Indians. Detectives in trench coats. An effervescent Mickey Rooney. He thinks of the views from their windows. Slow traffic, bent poplars, grey sky. It's May. It's bound to be raining. It'll probably be lashing down.

'Let's eat at the Ivy,' says Michael Redgrave. 'I haven't been for months.'

Noël's already dressed. He moves towards Michael and fastens the last three buttons of his shirt. 'The Ivy it is,' he says.

When Noël looks into the mirror he's slim in black and white. He lifts his chin. Pouts.

'Come on, beautiful,' says Michael. 'The cab will be waiting.'

'You know, I sometimes miss the war,' says Noël, filling his tortoiseshell case with fresh cigarettes. 'You looked particularly thrilling in uniform.'

Michael salutes. 'Would you like me to pipe you aboard the taxi?'

'I think you've done quite enough piping for one evening, thank you very much.'

As soon as Noël steps inside the restaurant he feels comfortable, despite the other diners breaking off their conversations, their eyes darting up from their plates, the women chewing on their lipstick. Michael greets one or two acquaintances.

'How's Rachel?' asks a woman.

'Very well, thank you,' says Michael. 'Couldn't be better.'

They sit in a quiet, unshowy corner. A familiar waiter offers them a menu.

'Still here, Charlie?' says Noël. 'I thought you were buggering off to Glasgow.'

'Glasgow fell through, sir,' he tells them quietly. 'The bastard went and got married.' He puts his hand to his mouth, turns bright pink, and starts backing away. 'I'm sorry, sir. I meant no disrespect to yourself, Mr Redgrave, sir. Really.'

'Oh stop grovelling and bring us the wine list,' says Noël. 'With eyes like yours, you could get away with murder.'

They order wine, chicken livers on toast, lobster bisque. 'Then I'll have the Barnsley lamb chop,' says Noël, which for some reason sets Michael giggling.

'I'm glad food's back,' says Noël. 'Rationing gave me such an enormous appetite. I was always thinking, what am I going to eat tonight? Worse than that – what am I going to drink?'

'It was the petrol that got me,' says Michael. 'I hated being tied to one place.'

'We managed.'

'I'll say.'

They eat quietly. Noël half listening to other conversations. A woman talking about her picture in *Vogue* magazine. A man ordering beefsteak. Another one missing his globetrotting son. The windows press lozenges of coloured light across the tabletops. He can see Charlie holding a woman's coat, his hands lost in the thick white fur of its collar.

'What do you suppose people think we talk about?' says Noël. His bisque tastes rich; the bowl is swimming with small clots of cream.

Michael looks up. Smiles. 'Films, I suppose. Show business.'

'Yes.'

'How's the soup?'

'Fishy.'

Later, when the cab has dropped Michael home and Noël is standing at his own bedroom window, he sees a man on the street devouring fish and chips from its flapping newspaper wrapping. Noël can still taste the lobster. The dense lamb chops with their piquant mint sauce. The man in the lamplight looks happy. He glances towards Noël and winks. He offers up a steaming chip. He bows. Blows on the chip. Licks his lips. Now, they're both laughing.

\* \* \*

145

Noël puts his head around the kitchen door. He'd expected complete disarray, but the room appears particularly tidy. Napkins sit like three white swans paddling across the worktop. The silver (now gleaming) has been arranged across a teacloth. Three pink lilies stand in a tall crystal vase. Three lilies for three lilies, thinks Noël. There's no sign of Patrice. Perhaps, he's run down to the News Shack for a copy of *Le Monde*, or *Larousse Gastronomique*.

He pours a large gin and tonic waiting for the bath to fill. The bubbles fizz and catch in his throat, causing a coughing fit, which makes him feel so drained he heaves himself into the bathroom and shuts off the running taps. 'I'm clean enough,' he pants. 'Better to be breathing than completely dirt-free.'

In the bedroom he finds his best Jamaican suit lying over the bed, the crisp shirt beneath the jacket, the silk socks at the hems. The large white underpants embarrass him. He pushes them under the trousers. Then he sits on the wicker chair, drinks more gin and tonic (carefully killing the bubbles with his tongue), and manages to get his breath back.

'Miguel? Is that you?' He can hear footsteps. If Miguel is back, Noël can simply hold out his arms and Miguel will dress him like a mannequin. Everything will be done with dignity and ease. There'll be no puffing and wheezing and buttons rolling over the floor tiles. No pants on back to front.

'Tomorrow, Boss!' comes the call from Patrice. 'Miguel will be back here tomorrow!'

'Of course he fucking will.'

Noël looks at the suit. The shirt. The socks make his heart sink. He might have to ask Patrice for help with the socks. He lifts up his feet. Are they clean enough? The nails could do with cutting.

Slowly, slowly, he pulls on the shirt. Right arm. Left. He sits and starts with the very last button. If he starts here, there's less chance of getting it wrong. He manages four before he takes another sip of his gin. They're small buttons. Pearly. He hates every last one of them.

When Patrice appears in the doorway, hesitating, Noël inadvertently blushes. He's managed his shirt, apart from the buttons nearest the collar which seem particularly tight and unyielding. He's kept the underpants he's worn all day and he's stepped into his trousers, but they remain pooled like ink at his ankles.

'Help, Boss?' says Patrice.

Noël nods.

'You know, Boss,' says Patrice, pulling up the trousers and fastening the buttons, 'you should have shouted me. I am here to help.'

'You are? You could have fooled me.'

Patrice is wearing a plain black suit. Noël can smell the soap on his neck. Toothpaste.

'Mr Payn and Mr Cole will be here in ten minutes, Boss,' Patrice says, brushing down the shoulders of Noël's ancient dinner jacket.

'Good,' he says, averting his eyes from the mirror.


'Has he been practising?' says Graham.

'Who?' Noël asks, looking at the birds circling the trees.

'Patrice, of course. Has he been grasping everything he can get hold of with a waiter's fork and spoon?'

Coley giggles. Noël's face doesn't stir. The birds move like puppets.

'I'd be hopeless,' says Graham. 'I wouldn't make it in a rib shack, never mind the Ritz.'

'Do rib shacks have waiter service?' says Coley. 'They're usually full of waitresses in gingham skirts with love bites on their necks.'

'It's just a meal,' says Noël. His iced cocktail glass drips water onto his trousers, which then mingles with the dropped ash from his cigarette. When he tries to brush it away, it makes a pale muddy puddle on his knee.

He can hear Graham and Coley chatting. He can hear Patrice moving the chairs inside the house. The birds have disappeared. He starts counting the leaves on the jasmine tree.

Patrice shows them inside. The table has been set with a starched white cloth and all the best china plates. The three pink lilies throw their deep heady scent into the dining room. A sprinkling of pollen. The napkins are swimming.

'Three isn't the usual number for a dinner party,' says Coley. 'It's usually four at the very least, unless it's *dinner à deux*.'

'It's not a dinner party,' says Noël, his thumb agitatedly clicking his cigarette lighter, which eventually sparks and dies. 'It's us. Having supper. Again.'

'It was your idea,' says Graham. 'You wanted to help Patrice.'

'Did I?' says Noël. 'Did I really?'

'Now let's be nice,' says Coley, throwing Noël a box of matches.

'Nice? I'm always fucking nice.' Noël takes a deep breath and smiles. A look passes between Graham and Coley that could set him back on edge, but he takes a sip of his rather good wine and simply lets it go. 'Now,' he says brightly, 'what do we know about silver service? Anything?'

Graham shrugs. 'They tend to hover,' he says.

149

'They put the food on your plate, give a stiff little nod and move on to your neighbour. Rather snooty if you ask me.'

'Don't they have to be right-handed?' says Coley. 'Is Patrice right-handed?'

'How should I know?' says Noël. 'I've no idea what that boy gets up to with his hands.'

'The food is always served from the left,' Coley adds. 'And it's always ladies first. Or the hostess. Or something.'

'That'll be me then,' says Noël with a pout.

'I must say, the cutlery looks right. And the glasses.' Coley lifts his water glass to the light. 'There's not a smudge on it. Not a fingerprint. Perfect.'

'All this fuss,' says Noël. 'Could we possibly talk about something else? Anything else. Please?'

'Like what?' says Graham. 'I think it's interesting.'

'Oh you do, do you?' Noël grins. 'I don't believe it. All those wasted years spent twiddling your thumbs when you could have been serving rare *filets mignons* at Rules, or flambéing *crêpes suzette*.'

Before Graham can say anything, Patrice appears. A smarter, brighter, more upright version of his usual self, he seems to glide between the furniture, coming up to Noël's left side, and as the dish is lowered, Noël moves his shoulder slightly, and between a fork and spoon a clump of marinated mushrooms are squeezed for dear life, arriving onto Noël's plate without incident. Patrice (panting ever so slightly) then retrieves a quarter of a lemon from the bowl which nudges the glistening brown fungi like a wide, witless smile. When he leaves the room (and Noël can now detect a very slight swagger in his hips), the three men are left almost speechless.

'Very smooth,' says Graham, shaking out his linen swan.

Noël spears a mushroom, looking towards the kitchen door. He thinks he can hear Patrice humming, though it might be the refrigerator.

'He's a natural,' says Coley. 'And he can cook.'

'They came out of a jar,' says Graham with a sniff. 'I'm certain of it.'

Coley, with a rather forced smile, starts chatting about a neighbour who fell and broke her ankle while shopping in Kingston. As he rattles on, Noël wonders if he should mention the coriander sticking in Graham's front teeth. Saying nothing, he concentrates on clearing his own plate. It's still early, not quite 7.30, but he can't help thinking how nice it would be to be eating his supper in bed.

When Patrice comes to clear the plates, Coley stops talking, and they look at their waiter with such unbridled admiration, he can't resist flashing them a smile.

The poached salmon would be a culinary work of art, jumping straight from the pages of an illustrated Julia Child or Fanny Craddock, if it wasn't for the effect of the black grape placed where the eyeball should have been. The way the grape has been angled makes the fish look slightly deranged. They try not to laugh out loud.

'Cucumber scales,' says Coley, pressing his fingers to his lips. 'How very lovely.'

Patrice opens his mouth as if to say something, then it appears he remembers that a silver service waiter should be dumb unless quizzed, and so he shuts it. Rule number two. Then Graham forgets to wait and refills his own wine glass. The salmon, like the mushrooms, is served with perfect grace. There are small boiled potatoes. Cold tomatoes. Peas.

'A summery combination,' says Coley. 'Very nice.'

Graham asks for mayonnaise. Patrice bows. When he gets to the kitchen they can hear him scrambling in the cupboards for the jar.

'That poor fish,' whispers Noël, 'looks like he's just swum out of Bedlam.'

By the time dessert is served, Patrice seems not to mind them pouring their own wine and water. There's only so much he can do. He looks very warm. He's lost a button from his jacket.

'I've always liked fruit salad,' says Graham, tucking in. 'It's refreshing.'

'We used to get it in tins. Do you remember? We'd have it with Carnation milk and there was only ever one cherry,' says Coley. 'We used to fight for the cherry.'

'I'd never fight for anyone's cherry.' Noël digs around for the mango. 'It's really quite undignified and rarely worth the bother.'

They take their brandy outside. The sky is streaked with a vibrant tangerine light and they stand for a minute looking at the clouds, the way they appear like long fraying islands.

'It's a shame Patrice didn't adopt his best waiter guise before you wrote him the reference,' says Coley, sitting down.

Noël stares at the red blistering end of his cigarette. The lights in Port Maria are just beginning to shine. 'We shouldn't get his hopes up,' he says.

When Noël goes to use the bathroom, he sees Patrice smoking in the kitchen, sitting on a worktop, his collar open, his black tie thrown across the newly washed plates. He turns to Noël and smiles. 'Thank you, Boss,' he says. 'I appreciate it. I appreciate everything.'

'Come and join us outside,' says Noël. 'Please. After all your hard work, I think you at least deserve a brandy.'

153

Ten minutes later, Noël emerges from the bathroom with his cuffs soaked from an accident with the cold tap. He sees Patrice sitting between Graham and Coley, laughing about something. The fireflies are starting to appear, hanging in the air like windblown fairy lights. Noël sits at the edge of the group, nursing his brandy glass, listening to them laughing about hotels, rude dinner guests, hot spilt soup. Coley has promised to type out a list of the usual French found on a restaurant menu. 'Anything I can think of,' he smiles. 'From *moules et frites* to *café au lait*.'

'My Uncle Autry was once a kitchen hand in Kingston,' says Patrice, now accepting a cigarette from Graham. 'The cook used to drink so much rum he'd sleep on a sack in the pantry. One sorry night he set the place afire. He'd left the batter pan burning on the stovetop.'

'Goodness. Did he die?' asks Graham, with his hand at his throat. His face is flushed. His brandy glass is empty.

'No, Boss.' Patrice shakes his head. 'He escaped, though his hair was burning like a beacon.'

'You must be very careful at the Ritz,' warns Coley. 'The hotel might be grand but it still has its fair share of hazards.' He turns towards Noël. 'Didn't you once know someone who'd cut his thumb off in their kitchen?'

154

'No.' Noël shakes his head. 'It was the Hilton, he'd trapped it in a cupboard, and it served him bloody well right. He had a very bad temper. He was always slamming things.'

Patrice pulls a face and throws a knowing look. Graham and Coley laugh with him – it's obviously a joke at Noël's expense. He pours more brandy. The fireflies dart between the wide creaking trees, the moon is like a plate; like something whittled out of bone.

'I think we'd better be going,' says Graham, glancing at his watch. 'If we don't go now, we'll never make it down the hill in one piece.'

They take their leave, Coley suddenly fussing over Miguel's imminent return. A vegetable delivery. Patrice is due back at Blue Harbour in the morning.

'Don't rush,' says Graham. 'You mustn't rush. Anytime before luncheon will do.'

Finally, they meander towards the car and wave their goodbyes. The headlights click on, obliterating the fireflies, catching a storm of small insects in the beams.

'Would you like helping to your room, Boss?' says Patrice, holding out his hand.

'No.'

'Would you like anything?'

'No.'

'Are you sure, Boss?'

'Quite fucking sure, Patrice, thank you.'

Noël listens to the whine and whirr of the insects. He pours another brandy. Lights another cigarette. Slumped in his chair he looks like a worn-out boxer. His arms ache with a sudden emptiness. Behind him, Patrice clatters around the house, whistling.

# TWO

# I

LIFE IS quiet. Nothing needs to be said. When he lifts himself from the bed he can already smell the fragrant bubbles in the steam. He strips off and walks like a saint of old with a towel around his waist. He lets it drop. He takes Miguel's calloused hand, lifts a knee, and when his left foot plunges into the water, it lands safely on a suctioned rubber mat. The temperature is perfect. The soap is close at hand. Bronnley's Pink Bouquet.

Later, while Miguel showers him lightly with talc and fastens every button, his wife, Imogen, fries bacon in the kitchen. By the time he steps outside, his breakfast plate, his tea, his newspapers and mail are sitting in the shade. After his last bite, the plate is removed. There is no sound from the kitchen. The pair move around in silence, like dancers with dusters on their shoes.

Days move slowly. The sky stretches above his head. It shifts through the hours from blue, to crimson, violet, to a deep pitch-black. He studies the cloud formations. The stars. Somewhere in the house there is a book of constellations. He has seen Orion's Belt.

Graham and Coley appear for cocktails most nights. They talk about Switzerland. David Niven. New wallpaper. In less than a month they will be looking at crisper blue skies. The cow bells will be clanking. They will eat schnitzel, casseroles, coddled eggs. Unless June is particularly kind, they will have their cocktails by the fireplace, or wrapped on the veranda, with the mountains in the distance, the snow achingly bright, the air so clean Noël is certain that it tastes of antiseptic.

Miguel takes their glasses. He brings a tray of clean ones. A bowl of pretzels. Stuffed green olives. He quietly backs out of sight.

'Happy now?' says Coley.

'How is Patrice?' asks Noël.

'Still whistling away,' says Graham. 'Still dancing to the radio in the kitchen.'

When they leave, Noël has an early night. He reads *The Railway Children*; a few pages are still coffee-stained, there's a flattened red ant on page 22. When he looks up he can hear himself breathing.

An owl startles him, flashing past the window. Saying nothing but 'Goodnight, Massa', Miguel leaves a cup of sweetened cocoa, two sleeping pills, and a glass of fresh water.

He reads a while longer, seeing the steam of the engine hovering at the platform, a portly Perks (now always Bernard Cribbins, much to Noël's annoyance) consulting his pocket watch. He blows his whistle, lowers the flag, and as the train pants out of the station, Trevor Howard appears, and Noël can hear his own voice crackling over the tannoy. David Lean sits on a tall pair of stepladders. By the waiting room, Celia Johnson is checking her stocking seams, straightening the right leg, rubbing at a mark on her shoe. A woman in a green paisley headscarf offers her a mirror. Mr Lean claps his hands and everyone looks towards him.

Miguel is a small slight man, yet he is able to manoeuvre his master with such dexterity that it appears to any passer-by that Sir Noël is capable of standing, of striding quite confidently from the car to the Lotus, where Graham and their friends the Barton-Coombs are waiting at a table. His armpits are sticky with sweat. Noël pats his right pocket, feeling the comfortable bulge of a handkerchief. As soon as he steps into the room the pianist in the corner (white jacket, wilting paper carnation) strikes up a brisk 'Mrs Worthington'. Noël drops his head a little. He waves his fingers to a few other diners. A woman in white starts coughing over her roast salt cod and yellow yam.

The Barton-Coombs, originally from Brighton, now ensconced in Saint Thomas, are an attractive couple in their sixties. Henry was a photographer, Laura his model. Henry stands as Noël comes towards them. He holds out his hand with a grin across his face.

'Long time, old friend, no see.'

'I'm a professional hermit,' Noël tells him, sitting down and quickly lighting a cigarette. 'Please don't take it personally.'

'We wouldn't,' says Laura. 'We hardly budge ourselves these days. Really. Gone are those long-winded club banquets. We no longer have to show our faces in all the right places. It's heaven.'

From the corner of his eye, Noël can see Miguel chatting to the familiar maitre d'. He finds his glasses and studies the gold-edged menu. It's a good restaurant. The chef has won awards. It's where the English and Americans go to eat Caribbean food on polished white plates, with orchids in bowls and squeaky-clean bathrooms. There is the genteel scraping of knives and forks. Low-volume chatter.

The pianist has moved onto a selection of traditional folk tunes. *Come, Mr tally man, tally me banana* . . .

Noël is hungry, but he isn't hungry enough. Everything looks complicated. The peanut noodles. Ackee and saltfish. The deep-fried breadfruit croquettes.

'I'll have the curried crab,' says Laura.

Noël likes the idea of the crab, but these days his stomach wouldn't stand for such a rich assault at lunchtime. He looks for the lightest-sounding dish. Red snapper salad.

'Of course we've talked over the phone, but we haven't seen you since your knighthood,' says Henry. 'Almost a year and a half. I wondered if we should bow to you or something when you came into the room.'

'I certainly wouldn't have stopped you,' says Noël. 'Though perhaps among friends it would have been a trifle excessive.'

'Well heavens, you waited long enough,' says Laura, slapping down her menu.

Graham looks uneasy but Noël rattles onwards. 'Lack of God, and the Other Thing,' he sniffs. 'Though, of course, it might have been the coconuts.'

'Coconuts?' says Laura. 'What on earth do you mean, coconuts?'

Graham laughs. 'When the Queen Mother came to lunch at Firefly, the meal was very hit and miss.'

'It was a hit,' says Noël. 'Eventually.'

'You ate coconuts?' Henry shakes open his napkin.

'No, they ate goat curry,' explains Graham; 'they used the coconuts as dishes. Of course Miguel was pleased. No washing-up.'

'The Establishment must have thought you'd turned into quite the Jamaican,' says Laura. 'No wonder they kept you waiting.'

'I *was* kept waiting,' says Noël, 'but I'm immensely proud. It was worth it.'

'Here, here!' Henry holds up his glass and they all follow suit, chinking crystal.

The waiter taking their orders has a long narrow face and scars on his hands. He appears dense with concentration, though they have to repeat what they'd like once or twice, and his pencil keeps scrubbing things out. 'Okra, sir?' he asks. 'Did you say okra?'

'No,' sighs Graham. 'No one wants okra, but we'll take another bottle of wine.'

'Now, sir, or with the meal.'

'Now,' says Noël, tapping his nails into the tablecloth. 'Please?'

The conversation turns to the maintenance of swimming pools. The words roll across him. The temperature of the water. Depth. The repair of concrete bases. Noël looks across the tables, between the waiters carrying trays. A blonde woman is lighting her friend's cigarette. In the corner a tank of blue and scarlet fish looks like an underwater window and he watches them swimming between the rods of coral, the floating strands of weed.

Noël would like to go to the bathroom. The door saying Rest Rooms looks too far away. He'd like a crutch, though he can hardly take Graham with him.

'Every time I look at the pool I think of Clemmie,' says Laura. 'Our granddaughter cut her head open, it was all a terrible mess.'

'It wasn't the pool's fault,' says Henry. 'It was Clemmie, messing around.'

'Four stitches.'

Graham winces. 'No scar, I hope?'

Laura shakes her head. 'No, they were very good in Kingston. Treated her like a queen.'

'Embroidered her like a rag doll,' says Henry. 'They gave her fruit pastilles but she hollered all the same.'

'Who wouldn't?'

Noël looks into his wine glass. The water pitcher. Any more liquid and he'll burst.

'Do excuse me,' he says, rising unsteadily to his feet. As he leans on the table he can feel his wrists bending, they send tremors into his elbows. His eyes look frantically for a clear route to the doors.

'Can you manage?' asks Graham.

'Of course.' He waves. 'Do carry on.'

Placing one foot in front of the other, he is aware of other lunch guests, the crackle of the air as he sidles past their tables. Halfway across the room he feels a hand grabbing at his elbow, he knows instinctively it's Miguel, and he knows Miguel will make such little fuss it will look like Sir Noel has bumped into an old acquaintance. 'Thank God,' Noël whispers. 'I thought you'd skedaddled. I almost didn't make it.'

The bathroom is empty. Noël goes into a stall while Miguel stays at the basins. He sits on the bowl, the relief is palpable, he almost feels like weeping. To the side of him a small frosted window has been pushed open half an inch. He can hear the bustle of Port Maria. The smell of the sea mingles with the cheap flowery scent of the air freshener. A radio plays something tinny and familiar.

As he pulls up his pants, he hears American voices, they've come banging into the bathroom, bullish and loud.

'I hate the way they look at me these days,' a man's saying. 'Like it's my fault I'm white. Like *I* tied them down.'

'What?' says his companion, whose voice sounds much the worse for drink. 'Whaddaya mean?'

'My family weren't slave owners,' he says. 'They were farmers in Ohio. There's no fucking blood on my hands.'

'No?'

'And I pay them wages.'

'No ya don't,' says the other man. 'Do ya?'

'I pay them for parking my car. For shining my shoes. For eating in places like this. Hell. I tipped the bellboy at the Myrtle more than was good for him. He'll probably be stoned. He'll probably spend the whole fucking lot of it on weed.'

'Ganja.'

'Shut up, Jimmy, you sound like one of them.'

Noël waits for them to leave. He leans against the door as they piss without talking and exit. He stays in the stall half a minute. A small pale gecko dances over the wall. He can hear Miguel running water. 'You all right, Massa?' he whispers. When Noël lifts the lock and steps outside, the first thing he sees is his own face in the mirror. His skin is mottled. Frayed. His forehead shines like an oriental buddha.

'You missed Mr Savvy,' says Graham, when Noël makes it back to the table and Miguel disappears into the hubbub at the bar. 'You missed the maitre d'.'

'Too bad,' says Noël, pouring himself another glass of wine. 'I'm sure Mr Savvy will get over it.'

Their food has arrived and Noël's red snapper is a giant combination of fish, and what he can only think of as tropical apparel. Half a pineapple has

167

been sawn into chunks and put back into its skin, complete with maraschino cherries and a jaunty paper umbrella. Grilled plantain sits next to a tower of grated coconut; the snapper is swimming, nay drowning, in curly green leaves that might or might not be lettuce. There are wheels of oranges. Shredded cucumber. Miniature fried potatoes and a pond of spiced mayonnaise. So much for 'light'. Attempting to make some dent in this Jamaican still life, he flakes off some of the fish, thinking of the salads in England, a few watery lettuce leaves, a sliced tomato, a hard-boiled egg and a beetroot; in Switzerland you would get even less.

'We were thinking of leaving,' says Laura.

'Oh?' Noël lifts his eyes and feigns a look of hurt surprise. 'Is the food really so bad? Or perhaps it's simply too overwhelming to be in such illustrious company?'

She smiles, wryly. 'Jamaica,' she says. 'We were thinking of leaving the island. It doesn't feel the same, now they've got their independence. I dare say it's all right and proper, but it worries me.'

'It's been almost ten years since independence,' says Graham. 'Hasn't it?'

'But she dreams of revolutions,' says Henry. 'She dreams of "Off with their heads!"'

'How exciting,' says Noël. 'Is there any knitting?'

168

'We decided against it,' Henry tells him. 'After all this time we'd probably die within a month of English weather. And I've never liked America. Not for the long term. Not really.'

'We get the best of both worlds,' says Graham. 'We'll be back in Montreux before you know it.'

'And what about the cold?' says Laura. 'Don't you feel it?'

'Oh, the sun can be dazzling,' says Graham, slicing into his chicken. 'We wear plenty of layers, and for the first few days we stay inside, drink lots of hot toddies and simply look at the world through the windows.'

'Do you ski?' asks Henry.

'Like demons,' says Noël.


Graham has left with Henry and Laura to spend an afternoon flopping by their swimming pool. Miguel is staying in town, collecting prescriptions and shopping. Sitting in the back of the car, Noël feels like he's swallowed a medicine ball. He shouldn't have succumbed to the chocolate rum tart and the ice cream. Even the brandy didn't help. He rests his chin in his hand and leans against the window. The road is bumpy, the air full of dust.

They come to a standstill outside Mrs V's Grocery Store. Mrs V is sitting on a stool on the pavement, fanning herself. She's a rotund woman with a circular face. She has gold hoops in her ears, her feet in rubber flip-flops, her splayed toenails painted a vivid shade of blue.

'Sorry, Massa.' The driver turns his head. 'All jammed up today.'

Noël says nothing. He's glad when they've moved a few yards forward, when they've passed the grocer's with its towers of canned tuna and tubs of cornmeal porridge. He does not want to think about food. He sees a small boy with sticking plasters on his knees, playing a battered tin drum, his T-shirt so small it rides up his ribcage. They stop. The boy looks towards the car, wide-eyed, his hands still intent on the drumming. In front of them horns start blaring, doors are slamming and a cacophony of voices rise from open windows.

'Something must have happened, Massa, not just heavy traffic, an accident, I think.'

Noël groans. His head throbs in time to the drumming. A cockerel runs squawking between some empty cardboard crates. Music pulsates. He can hear at least three different reggae tunes.

His driver opens his door and steps into the heat. The sunlight catches on the rear-view mirror, shooting arrows into the car. Noël's chest feels tight, and in a panic he starts circling his ankles. A fly the size of his thumbnail makes a dizzying entrance, throwing itself across the interior as Noël tries to bat it away.

'Could we turn around?' Noël opens his window and shouts to his driver, now leaning on the bonnet. With all the commotion the driver doesn't hear and Noël sinks back into the vinyl with a sigh. Trying to relax, trying not to fret about the heat, the people gawping, the tightness in his chest, he runs through old lines in his head. He starts with *Hay Fever*, but he only makes it to *The poor girl's potty!* before the driver comes slamming inside, saying the police are up front and seeing to the matter.

'We will be stopped and started with hand signals,' he says. 'Human traffic lights.'

They move slowly. Noël closes his eyes as they come to another standstill, jerking wide awake when he hears the passenger door open and a man jumps inside, slamming the door behind him. Startled, Noël looks towards the driver, who seems unconcerned, scratching the back of his head. Noël pulls himself into the corner, his heart beating nineteen to the dozen; he can almost see it pushing through his shirt.

'All right, Boss?'

'Fucking hell, Patrice, do you want to give me a heart attack?'

'Sorry, Boss. I was waiting for the bus, and the policeman said there was no chance of a bus. I tried tapping on the glass but you looked like you were sleeping. Smoke, Boss?' he says, offering a crushed packet of Marlboros. 'Go on, Boss. I've plenty. Help yourself.'

'Thank you.' Noël's hand is shaking as he takes the cigarette and lights it.

'I don't know.' Patrice looks unruffled, like he jumps into cars every day. 'What's with all the fussing?' he says, smoke billowing from his nostrils as Noël pats his weeping forehead with his handkerchief. '*Tsk*. You wasn't even moving.' He sits with his knees wide open. He's wearing jeans and a pale denim shirt. 'You been out, Boss?' he asks.

'What do you think?' says Noël.

'You been somewhere nice?'

'Yes. A restaurant,' he says. 'With Mr Payn and friends.'

'Which restaurant? Did you go to the Bay?'

Noël shakes his head – he can see the rest room, the maitre d', his giant red snapper, yet he has no idea what the restaurant was called, and his friends have disappeared inside a thick grey fog. 'Just the usual place,' he stutters, and thankfully Patrice quickly changes the subject.

'Joe is now in London,' he says, looking at his

over-large wristwatch. 'Right at this very minute my cousin might be walking around Brixton, or he might be passing Piccadilly, or the Buckingham Palace. He might see the Queen waving through one of her windows.'

Noël smiles. He has a vision of a white glove lifting a dusty net curtain. Patrice stopping at the gates. Waving back. 'How's he doing? Have you heard?'

'Only a postcard, Boss. The postcard said: "I've landed." Two words, that's all. It was a very plain postcard. White, Boss. No picture. No sky with its painted-out rainclouds. I was very disappointed.'

They reach the junction where an overweight policeman stands behind a barrier, growling, waving traffic through. At the side of the road the debris of a car sits glittering in a lake of shattered glass. 'Cars,' says Patrice. 'More trouble than they're worth.'

The driver laughs. 'You want to get out and walk, Patrice Clarke?'

Patrice rolls his eyes. 'Nah, I'm all right sitting. The afternoon is baking. You been doing your walking, Boss?' he asks.

'On and off.'

'On and off isn't good enough, Boss! You need your Patrice to chivvy you along!'

173

'I'm not here to be pestered,' says Noël.

Through the window the edge of the road appears to be shimmering, floating higher than the pavement. A bar-room has a dead fluorescent parrot on its wall and signs saying: FAMOUS COCONUT SHRIMP, MUSIC, BEER, WINE HOUSE. Noël would like to fart, but he manages to keep hold of the gas until an ambulance starts wailing and he can release it without the fear of being heard. Patrice is humming, clicking his tongue against his teeth. He suddenly reaches out through his window and starts waving wildly to a woman in a bright green dress.

'Yoo hoo! *Yoh!* Monique!' He laughs. 'My sister!'

'Your long-lost sister, I presume?' says Noël, glancing backwards.

'She lives in Port Maria. Why would she be lost?'

Of course Noël knows Port Maria and he knows they are less than ten minutes from Blue Harbour, where Patrice will roll out of the car and saunter through the gates, whistling, singing, or snapping his fingers to the music in his head. He will go into the kitchen where he'll drink a Coca-Cola and start peeling the potatoes, 'in less than ten seconds flat'. When he's finished for the day, he might beg a lift to one of the bars, where they play reggae, or have flickering televisions. He might go dancing. Drinking. He might go looking for girls.

174

The car stops. The sun throws sparks across the rooftops and when Noël lets his eyes drop it almost looks like rain. Patrice holds out his hand.

'See you, Boss,' he says, a cigarette hanging from his lips. 'Thanks for the ride.'

His hand is warm and Noël can still feel the weight of it as Patrice slams the door and walks through the gates, stopping to turn, the sun sparks flying at his shoulders. He makes an elaborate bow, like an Elizabethan courtier, or an actor. Noël lifts his hand as the car moves away.

A Suite
The Ritz Hotel, London
Autumn, 1954

COWARD *sits on a red velvet sofa adjacent to a white marble fireplace (lit). Vases are dripping with expensive hothouse flowers. A butler serves drinks. Scotch. A bone-dry sherry.* SMITH *appears, breathless. His mackintosh is patterned with raindrops. He's a cub reporter, nineteen years old. His tuft of blond hair has been hastily rubbed dry in the corridor (a cleanish pocket handkerchief).* SMITH *is small and wiry, boyish, slightly nervous. He moves as if his shoes are pinching. He grips his pencil hard.*

COWARD: So, you're the *Express*?

SMITH: I am today, sir. Yes.

COWARD: No recorder?

SMITH [*looking woefully at his pencil*]: I'm sorry. I was too late, sir. They'd gone.

COWARD: Gone? Gone where?

SMITH: With the other reporters, sir.

COWARD: Well there's nothing you can't do with a pencil. Cigarette?

SMITH: No, thank you, sir. I don't.

COWARD: There's no need for 'sir'. I'm not Mr Beaverbrook. It's Noël.

SMITH: Yes, sir. Noël.

COWARD: You found me all right then? I'm usually at the Dorchester. I prefer it. I sang there during the war. They're always very kind to me, they have never forgotten it. But their suites were unavailable so the Ritz had to do. Are you writing all this down?

SMITH [*reddens*]: I didn't think we'd started . . .

COWARD: Well, we have now. Fire away.

SMITH: You were a great success at the Café de Paris last week. A sell-out. All the stars were there. Do you think you'll concentrate on cabaret from now on?

COWARD: Of course not. Why should I?

SMITH: Your appearance [*he stumbles*] seemed so much more . . .

COWARD: Spit it out. What?

SMITH: Assured. More successful than your recent productions. [*He flicks through his notes.*] *Ace of Clubs*, for example . . .

COWARD: Was years ago. 1949.

SMITH: *After the Ball* . . .

COWARD: Was a delightful entertainment, based on *Lady Windermere's Fan*.

SMITH: Didn't audiences think it was a little . . . old-fashioned?

COWARD: On the nights I was there, they applauded very loudly. We had at least one standing ovation. Now, what are you trying to say?

SMITH: That perhaps you have a new type of audience?

COWARD: Of course I have a new type of audience. It's growing! People young and old are discovering the delights of Noël Coward every day.

SMITH: What do you think of the critics?

COWARD: I think of them very little, as a matter of fact.

SMITH: And away from the theatre. Do you have a happy private life?

COWARD: Yes. I'm really very fortunate in that respect.

SMITH [*blushing*]: Do you have someone special to share it with?

COWARD: I do indeed, but there's always room for one

more. You have a very sweet face and I suppose you find me devastatingly attractive?

SMITH: Well I . . .

COWARD: Don't be coy. We could slip into the bedroom. No one need know.

SMITH [*dropping his pencil*]: I'm getting married, Mr Coward. Next June.

COWARD: Marriage? You look far too young for all that. You shouldn't tie yourself down. Life is full of opportunities. Especially for a reporter. A press card will get you into all sorts of interesting places.

SMITH [*loosening his collar*]: Is there anyone else you'd like to work with?

COWARD: I'm rather fond of 'me'.

SMITH [*confused*]: You'd like to work with yourself?

COWARD: Yes. You could watch me. Then I could watch you. Or we could synchronise.

SMITH [*scrambling to his feet and looking for the butler*

179

*who had taken his coat*]: And what are your plans for the future?

COWARD: The immediate future? [*He pats the cushion at his side. Winks.*] Come a little closer. We could smooch.

SMITH: I'm afraid I have to be going. Deadlines.

COWARD: You didn't touch your sherry. Not a drop. What a shame.

SMITH *limps towards the door as the butler appears with his rather creased mackintosh.*

COWARD [*taking a sip of his Scotch*]: Now you behave yourself, Mr *Express*. And remember, tempting though it might be in that mackintosh . . .

SMITH: Sir?

COWARD: Try not to expose yourself – it's particularly unbecoming in the rain.

SMITH *Exits* [*quickly*].

Miguel's wife has brought him Pepto-Bismol. He sips it like a liqueur in the sitting room with the tray-table across his knees. He can feel his stomach bubbling.

'Put Chopin on,' he tells her. 'He might calm things down or kill me.'

Soundlessly, Imogen riffles through the records. When the needle lowers and the music starts, she leaves. Noël assumes she's doing other work in the kitchen, upstairs, or outside, but he hears nothing, only the rise and fall of the piano and the very slight hissing of the dust.

The music makes him think of a crowded room. It's the tail-end of the forties. People are moving with their arms stiffly gripped to their sides. In a mist of Evening in Paris and Park Drive cigarettes they are shuffling around a small parquet dance floor. Above their heads giant chandeliers drip their glass pendants like strings of frozen rain, and as he backs into a corner he starts counting the drops, ignoring the yells and waving fingers, the tugs at his sleeve, the fawning.

Everyone is more or less familiar. The host in naval uniform. His wife. The ingénue in her dress of fluffy virgin white (all for show, she's had at least three men from the cast that he knows of). His own 'made-up' family are chatting at a table. Graham. Joyce Carey. Gladys Calthrop. Lorn Loraine. The chandelier is complicated. He makes it to forty-three before Graham stands up and looks in such desperate need of his company that he abandons the shivering glass and, pressing between elbows, uniforms and waiters with quaking trays, he finds himself at the table. Graham's smiling. Noël takes a sip or two of his wine, but then as he's starting to relax he has a familiar feeling in the pit of his stomach. On cue the host hits a glass with a teaspoon and calls for silence. When the chatter has subsided and the music whines to a stop, the host waves in their direction, inviting Mr Coward to oblige them at the piano. 'I wonder,' he says, 'if you could possibly entertain us with a small repertoire of your songs?' The room breaks into thunderous applause. Noël makes his way across to the piano. It's a good piano. A Steinway. He opens the lid. Takes a deep breath. Rubs his clammy fingers. Plays.

'No more trips out,' he tells Miguel that night. 'No more restaurants, or barber's shops, or a paddle on the beach. I'll be back among the cuckoo clocks before I know it. I need to be on top form for the fucking photographers. Look at me. I feel bloated. Distended. That red fucking snapper's still snapping.'

'More Pepto-Bismol, Mr Coward?'

'Never mind the pink emulsion, fetch me a Martell. I'll have Martell instead of cocoa. My stomach needs tranquillity.'

'A little ginger with the brandy, sir?'

Noël throws *The Railway Children* at him. It hits him hard on the side of his face. Miguel puts his hand to his cheekbone.

'For crying out loud don't look so cowed, it was hardly *War and* fucking *Peace*!'

'No, sir.' He's bleeding where the corner cut into him. He dabs it with a tissue from his pocket.

'Straight Martell. No ginger. No fucking messing about.'

'Yes, sir.'


Lying in bed he looks at the mound of his stomach sitting underneath the sheets. An igloo. A basin. A mosque. He rests his brandy glass on it. He tries to fart. Nothing. Like an expectant mother he rubs his hand across the contours. He presses at it. If he lifts the sheet he will see all its pale glory. The fine grey hairs. The perfect impression of his top trouser button. A mole.

He looks at *The Railway Children*. There's a spot of blood on it so he swaps it for *The Wouldbegoods*. His glasses keep slipping down his nose. He'd like another brandy but he doesn't have the strength to shout for Miguel. He looks at the pills. He's always exhausted. Sleep should come easier than this.

At the last minute he pulls out his teeth and drops them into the tumbler with its effervescent tablet.

He can feel his lips curling inwards, like a turtle. When he clicks off the light the world is very quiet. Even the crickets have ceased their constant racket. There is no clattering downstairs. No music. No whistling. Nothing. For once it unnerves him. Shouldn't something be creaking? What about the water in the cistern? The infernal feral cat? He counts to ninety-two. Recites some French. He hums 'I Travel Alone' and as he's still awake he veers into several lively medleys from *Salad Days*.

## 2

MIGUEL SETS up the television in the sitting room. The reception is notoriously bad, but by balancing the aerial on a window frame, the picture isn't too stormy and the sound is more or less perfect. Noël sits in his dressing gown with the TV guide open at his side. At ten past two JBC are showing *Jailhouse Rock* and a glimpse of Mr Presley swivelling his hips is worth the inconvenience of the fuzzy black and white.

He watches an advertisement for toothpaste. For something that loosens your hair. He sees the titles. '*Starring Elvis Presley*'. Ten minutes later he's asleep and even the music doesn't rouse him. When he wakes, a man in a badly fitting suit is interviewing Clancy Eccles.

'What happened to Elvis? I missed him.'

'You ever meet Elvis, Massa?' asks Miguel, dismantling the aerial.

'No, more's the pity. Why did you let me sleep through it? There's nothing on all day but politics and *Gilligan's Island*. I could have slept like a log through that.'

'I was in the garden. I was pulling out the weeds on the footpath.'

'Still,' pouts Noël. 'Elvis.'

Later, when he's eating a bowl of vegetable soup (nothing too heavy today, but he does manage a roll and some butter, a generous slice of raisin cake), he thinks about a boy he met who looked like Elvis Presley. He'd asked him to demonstrate one or two moves with his pelvis. The boy had obliged, but he didn't have the rhythm, and when he'd opened his mouth, he spoke in broken English.

'From Rimini,' he'd said. 'Tourist.'

They'd spent the day together in a hotel room, managing the language barrier with a phrase book and Noël's smattering of Italian. He had marvelled at the boy's perfect lips, his pomaded black quiff and long girlish hands, but after the sex all the boy had seemed interested in was shopping.

'You're a gigolo,' Noël had told him.

'*Si*,' he'd said, handing Noël a leather jacket. '*Si*.'

Noël's heart sinks at the sight of the packing cases. He likes Switzerland. He likes his chalet, his study, the view from the windows, but it's such a fag getting there. Everything's an effort, even when most of it's done by Coley, or Graham. Noël has to follow them. He has to show the world his best side. The quips with the air stewards. The newspapermen.

Lying in the sun he's already thinking of lambs-wool jumpers and his thickest Argyll socks. He thinks about working. He panics. He hasn't even written in his diary.

'I can't settle,' he tells Miguel. 'I feel . . . unnerved.'

'Just relax, Mr Coward. Have a glass of rum punch. You are still in Jamaica. You haven't left us yet.'

'Where's Mr Payn?' he asks.

'Blue Harbour, Massa.'

'What's he doing there?'

'I don't know. Should I get him?'

'No,' snaps Noël. 'Of course not.'

He stares at the swimming pool through his sunglasses. The water looks like glass. He can feel tears behind his eyes but when Miguel reappears with a jug of rum punch he grins like a loon and says, 'Ain't Jamaica grand?'

Forty minutes later, with Captain Morgan's confidence, Noël looks at his feet already strapped firmly into his sandals. At the back of the house he can see a pattern of shade. He thinks of the walk. Of his sluggish circulation. He should walk. Of course he should walk. He doesn't need to be chivvied. He heaves himself vertical and shuffles into the garden, short-cutting through a bush that reminds him of brambles.

'You need something, Massa?' Miguel is already at his side. 'You want more ice? More cigarettes?'

'I'm going for my walk,' says Noël. 'If I'm not back by suppertime send out the troops.'

'But, Massa, it is not a good time for walking. You shouldn't be going out there on your own.'

'It's hardly the Blue Mountains,' he says, brushing Miguel's hand away from his elbow. 'I'm not after planting my flag at the summit. I'll only be gone ten fucking minutes. Anyway, it's doctor's orders.'

'You need to take water, Mr Coward.'

'I did without it the last time.'

'I'll come with you. Yes, Massa?'

'Only,' says Noël, 'if you have to.'

Shoulders as far back as they'll go, Noël tells himself that walking is nothing, it's the easiest thing in the world, and as he was a precocious tot he's been walking for far longer than most people his age, and instead of thinking about it, he should just get on and do it.

By the time they reach the first bend in the lane, his knees are throbbing and his chest is starting to ache. Noël looks down. Did these legs really dance around a stage, nimble as you like? Did they jump

188

onto surfboards, waterskis, trolley cars? He stops to catch his breath. For a minute the world looks out of focus. He can hear a pounding. It takes him a while to realise the pounding is actually his heartbeat.

'You're very quiet,' he tells Miguel. 'What happened to the chatter?'

'You don't like me to chatter, Massa. You always say it annoys you.'

'Well today I need chatter. Say something.'

'Like what?'

'I don't know. Any fucking thing. What about the other week? Where did you bugger off to again?'

'I went to see my cousin, Massa. He lives in Montego Bay.'

'Very nice spot.'

'Yes, Massa.'

'Anything else?'

'He is ill, Massa.'

'That's a shame.'

The pounding continues and though Noël supposes he should be glad of it, he's just waiting for the hammering to stop. He imagines the blood sitting in his chest. If the pounding stops will he drop down dead? And how on earth will Miguel drag him home?

'Is that it?' says Noël, lighting a cigarette. 'Is that all you have to say about your cousin?'

'Yes, Massa.'

189

'So he's boring?'

'No, Massa. He is dying.'

'Shit.'

His feet are slipping and sliding. The ground is dry, scattered with broken twigs and small red stones. Miguel, who could skip ahead, who could run to Blue Harbour in less than ten minutes, stays close at hand, though Noël is certain he can hear him tutting and sighing, dragging his feet like a child.

'You want to go back?' says Noël.

'How are you feeling?' he asks. 'Are you feeling okay, Massa?'

'I'm as fit as a fiddle. I'll count another twenty-five steps then we'll turn around and whistle our way home.'

'Whistle, Massa?'

'I was joking. Talking will do.'

'Talking, Massa?'

Noël slaps his own damp forehead. 'Here we go again . . . Montego Bay,' he says, grinning through his teeth. 'How did it look?'

'Same as always, Massa.'

'I thought you'd say something like that.'


Sweat pouring, limbs like lead, he drags himself upstairs. He needs his bed for at least half an hour. Imogen has already started folding his shirts and piling them onto a chair. His Jamaican clothes are hanging in the wardrobe

190

for the days he has left, and they will stay here, with the camphor balls and cedar blocks. Where else could he wear such light garish shirts or such bleached tatty shorts? He runs his hands across them. Everything looks shapeless. Loose. The shoulders seem to be shrugging at him. He lies on the bed and places his hands across his chest. A medieval monument. When he closes his eyes he can still see the shirts. The saggy-looking cardigans. The trousers with the easy-to-wear elastic sewn into their waistbands. Really, he could weep. Again.

'Anderson & Sheppard,' he tells his driver. It's a drizzly London day. 1938. The windows are steamed and Noël clears a patch with his hand to see the Georgian houses, the shops with the uniformed doormen.

His car stops at the kerb and when he steps outside, he can see the turning heads, the nudges and stares, even from the most respectable-looking pedestrians. As soon as he enters the shop he feels a frisson of excitement, half remembering the days when he'd stuff things up his coat sleeves.

The floorboards creak. He moves through the front of the shop where women and children are allowed to wait. Today, a woman sits with her head down, reading *David Copperfield*. The air smells of cloth. In the lamplight he can see the flecks of stray lint and cotton. Mr Pritchard comes to meet him, his hand already extended, his brass-edged measure hanging around his collar like a charmer with his snake.

'Mr Coward,' he says. 'We've made tea. What a dreadful, gloomy day.'

His measurements are taken swiftly, without comment, in front of a crackling fire. A table to the side holds the tea things, a plate of plain biscuits. Before the samples are shown, Noël takes a cup of tea, leafing through one of the magazines, feeling the heat of the fire on his ankles.

He chooses a grey herringbone, a hand-loomed Shetland tweed. The cloth consultant is on hand to talk about the climate and how the cloth was made. They talk about design. Both the consultant and Mr Pritchard are focused on the tailoring, 'Double-breasted, of course.' No mention is made of the theatre.

He tells his driver to take him to Harrods. He feels like spending some money. For almost two hours he wanders the floors in a world of his own, picking out ties, tie clips, soft woollen scarves, Moroccan leather slippers, a dozen other things. He sniffs so many bottles of scent they all meld into one floral-amber bouquet. He lifts teacups that have been hand-painted in Kyoto. Engraved silver fish knives.

At the stationery counter he bumps into John Gielgud and Noël offers to drive him home, the car slicing through the drizzle, the headlights glowing.

'I actually like driving through the city in the rain,' says Noël.

'Still, I hate it when it hammers down. I have a large collection of umbrellas,' John tells him. 'Some I've acquired. Most I've lost. When the sun actually chooses to make an appearance, one doesn't like to walk with a brolly in one's hand.'

'I do,' says Noël. 'I use them like weaponry. If I see an enemy approaching, I can happily fend them off.'

'An enemy?'

'Oh, you know,' says Noël, 'hacks and reporters. If I saw that cunt Beaverbrook walking towards me, the brolly would be up quick as you like, rain or no rain.'

The tyres hiss along the road. People are sheltering under awnings, they stand looking at the mannequins in brightly lit shop windows, then they make a dash for it, and Noël can almost hear their stockings squelching inside their leaking shoes.

'All this grey,' sighs John. 'London looks ancient.'

'I dream about the sunshine.'

'It's almost November.'

'I said sunshine,' says Noël, offering John a cigarette. 'It doesn't have to be English.'


'Elvis was on TV today,' says Noël. 'Elvis!'

'Really?' says Graham.

'I missed it.'

'Never mind. Our flight's at 11 a.m.,' Graham tells him. 'Everything's been arranged.'

'When for?'

'I told you five minutes ago. Next Thursday.'

'Thursday?'

'We like flying on Thursdays.'

'These days, I'm not sure I like flying at all. I'd like to close my eyes, click my fingers and find myself tucked in my little Swiss bed.'

'If only it were all that easy,' says Graham, folding the timetable. 'We have a chair on standby. We had to order it.'

'Fuck the chair. I can walk.'

'On standby. Just in case.'

'I know what standby means,' says Noël. 'You don't have to explain words to me. I'm not completely gaga. I can walk. I walked today.'

'To the pool? To the fridge? The walk to the plane can be quite a long stretch. There are stairs.'

'I'll have you know I walked down the fucking lane and back.'

'How far down the lane?'

'Far enough, thank you.'

Noël is lying in bed. He's had his supper (alone) on a tray. His knees are still throbbing but he says nothing. Graham, suntanned in white linen, looks particularly perky tonight.

'I've been on a bit of a diet,' he says. 'Can you tell?'

'Fuck off with your diets. Are you trying to torment me? Well, thanks for making me feel particularly elephantine. Some friend you are.'

'You're not like an elephant, and, anyway, I've only lost half an inch.'

'Where from?' says Noël. 'Your cock?'

Ignoring this last remark Graham moves towards the window. He lifts his arm, puts it against the wall and leans on it. The back of his neck is the colour of toast. Noël can see the line where his hair has been cut. He can feel tears pricking at his eyes.

'It's been like paradise,' says Noël.

'What has?'

'Jamaica. Here.'

'It still is,' says Graham. 'Isn't it?'

'I remember the first time we saw it. The first time we flew in from New York. I couldn't believe it was mine.'

Graham turns. 'There'd been a blizzard,' he says. 'New York was covered in ice.'

'Have you been happy here? Are you glad I found it?'

'Of course,' he says, pulling at his earlobe. 'Of course I'm glad you found it.'

# 3

LEANING AGAINST the kitchen sink he counts off the days on the calendar. Less than a week before they have to leave for Switzerland. He turns the tap and feels the lukewarm water running through his fingers. He can hear the feral cat moaning and mewling outside. It's been a quiet day. He pushes his wet hands across the balding dome of his head. He throws a little water down the open neck of his shirt. He glances at the clock. It's gin time.

Miguel and Imogen have left him alone. They've turned down his bed and arranged his pyjamas. He has assured them he is capable of getting himself into the bedroom and if he needs any assistance he will call them. He slams the ice tray onto the counter. A few cubes splinter and crack. He slams it again and again until the ice is sitting in a small wet pool and he has to brush off some stale breadcrumbs before throwing the cubes into his glass.

Outside the lanterns have been lit. Citronella candles sit in what appear to be jam jars but which are something Coley went and paid an arm and a leg for in Kingston. 'They have etchings,' he'd said, holding them aloft. 'Palm fronds and flowers.'

'Which happen to be invisible to the naked eye,' said Noël. 'You've been had. They're cast-offs from the Goldenglow jam company. You can smell the mixed-fruit jelly. You can see where the labels have been.'

He sits in a circle of light. The moths are waltzing. The air is suddenly still. With his gin and tonic in one hand, a cigarette in the other, he feels at peace with the world. Swifts dip and dive into the swimming pool. He thinks of the swallows in Kent. He'd watch them from the kitchen window, their pale feathers glowing, their long dark tails streaming in the wind.

The silence is broken by two long whistles. Noël starts. He can feel his heart risking everything, doing somersaults over his ribcage.

'Hey, Boss! Hey, Boss! *Yoo-hoo!*'

Noël smiles with relief. Patrice. He takes another sip of gin. Adjusts himself.

Patrice slopes into the garden. 'Only me, Boss. No heart attack now. Okay?'

'I'm not promising anything,' says Noël. 'What do

you want? Aren't you supposed to be at Blue Harbour? Has Mr Payn let you out?'

'I've finished work, Boss,' he sings. 'I've finished here for ever.' He lifts his arms, waves his fingers and dances.

Noël sits a little straighter. 'What do you mean? Don't tell me the Ritz lower management have wired for you already?'

Patrice pulls up the nearest wicker chair. 'No, Boss, not the Ritz. From the Ritz I've heard nothing.'

'I'm not *completely* surprised.'

'But I have heard from Joe, Boss, and Joe has found me employment.'

'Doing what?'

'Working in a restaurant. A small place in Brixton. It's called Ma Henry's. Ma Henry has promised me a job in the kitchen. My friend Victor has got me a passage on the Jamaica Producer boat. All I have to do is load crates and label bunches of fruit.'

'When?'

'Tomorrow night, Boss. I'm here to say goodbye.'

'Oh. You'd better get us a drink then. I was on gin and tonic, but I think I'll switch to brandy.'

'Martell, Boss?'

'Martell, Patrice.'

He can hear Patrice whistling as he goes inside the house. It sounds like 'Mad About the Boy', but he knows that can't be right.

'Cheers, Boss.' Patrice holds out his glass.

'Cheers.'

'I've been saying goodbye all day,' Patrice tells him. 'I've left my mother baking, packing and weeping.'

'It's all a bit sudden,' says Noël, offering him a cigarette. 'I expect she's in shock.'

'Oh, she's happy for me really. England. She knows it's what I've been wanting.'

'Is it?' Noël raises his left eyebrow and takes a sip of brandy. 'To leave this beautiful island to go pot-washing in Brixton?'

'It's a start, Mr Coward. And on my day off, I'll be able to present myself in person to the Ritz.'

They sit for a minute, watching the moths moving in and out of the light.

'London Pride,' says Noël.

'I know about London,' says Patrice. 'I've spent every night this week reading a book. I couldn't put it down. *Looking at London* by Alfred J. Pointer. Have you heard of it, Boss?'

Noël shakes his head.

'Mr Cole lent it to me. Over a hundred pages. Fully illustrated. I read all about the Thames. The Marble Arch. The men with the fuzzy black hat things.'

'You mean the Grenadier Guards of Her Majesty.'

'And then there was a theatre with your name on it. Page 45. "The Glorious West End". I kept looking at that name written out in sparkling light bulbs. That's the Boss, I thought. The man who likes soft-boiled eggs. Martell. The man who shouts at me for singing and for dancing to the radio. Did you buy another radio, Boss? The other one was smashed to smithereens.'

'I have no radio,' Noël tells him. 'I have no need of a radio.'

'Not even for the weather reports?'

'Especially not for the weather reports.'

Patrice sits back. He makes a bright orange circle with his smouldering cigarette. He crosses his feet at his ankles. 'You are different here, Boss. No light bulbs. No crowds. In Jamaica you are a different Noël Coward.'

'And how would you know?'

'I've read things. I've heard. In England I am going to be a different Patrice Clarke.'

'What's wrong with this one?'

Patrice chews his lips. He tells Noël that when he eventually arrives in London, shivering and wrapped in his muffler, he will be a stranger to everyone but Joe. He won't be known for the time he fell from his brother's fishing boat and almost drowned looking for the watch he had stolen that morning from his father. Or for the girl called Cecile who'd stabbed her arm with a steak knife because he wouldn't take her dancing. Or for crying like a baby when his old dog died.

200

'Or for being a servant, Mr Coward. I might even change my name like Mr Cole. I will call myself Smith. Or Brownlow. Something very English.'

'There's nothing wrong with being Jamaican.'

'But you're glad you're an Englishman?' he says, quickly draining his glass.

Noël smiles. 'Of course. I'm Sir Noël Coward. I'm very patriotic.'

'What was it like?' asks Patrice. 'Kneeling for the Queen?'

Noël can feel his cheeks burning. He can see himself, fumbling, having to go down on both knees as he'd never balance on one knee alone. The look of relief on the Queen's face when he'd managed to right himself and leave the room without falling. The medal in the small black box.

'It was a very proud moment,' he says, his hand reaching for the brandy bottle. 'I couldn't have been happier.'

Patrice takes the bottle from him and pours them both a drink. The candles quiver in the jam jars. The pale yellow flames leap inside the glass. 'You have always been generous,' he says. 'Always.'

'It's only brandy.'

'And you pay very good wages, you are famous for it, my father helped dig out your swimming pool, I'm told we lived like kings for weeks.'

'That was over twenty years ago.'

'My mother still speaks of it.'

'Well.'

'I am going to be a generous boss when I've made my fortune in London.'

'The streets aren't paved with gold. The streets are usually filthy.' Noël closes his eyes. A man in a grey balaclava lifts an ashcan onto his shoulder. A bony black cat goes skulking over a wall. There are piles of sodden newspapers. Cinders. Tin cans. A woman beats her rug leaning out of an upstairs window.

'I don't mind the dirt, Mr Coward. Kingston is full of it.'

They drink in silence. Between the trees, the fireflies move in fast glowing ribbons. Noël taps his foot; he can hear himself breathing.

'Are you mad with me, Boss?' says Patrice.

'Why should I be mad?'

'Because I'm leaving Blue Harbour. Because I am going to London tomorrow.'

'No,' says Noël. 'I really couldn't give a shit.'

Patrice wobbles inside to find another bottle of brandy. Noël's world is starting to slide. The water in the swimming pool should be sloshing over the side. The moon sears his eyes. The stars are dripping into the vast jet sky.

'Let me offer some advice,' says Noël, accidentally

dropping his cigarettes at his feet. Patrice scrambles to pick them up, he stands swaying like a tall piece of sugar cane, with the packet in his hand.

'More advice, Boss?'

'When you get to London, you should be yourself. People always prefer the genuine article.'

Patrice falls heavily into the chair. 'Unless,' he says, fumbling with his lighter, 'unless they are watching a play.'

'In which the characters *appear* as the genuine article.'

'So the actor playing a duke might be a drug-peddling gangster in real life,' he says, managing to light their cigarettes with the smallest orange flame. 'And his family might be starving in the gutter, but as long as he rolls his "r"s and remembers all his lines, then everything's all right?'

'Well, there's more to it than that,' says Noël, 'but I think you have the gist of it.'

'Play-acting,' says Patrice, crossing his legs and staring at the sky.

'Yes, but it's given us both a living, so let's thank God for that curtain going up.'

Patrice cocks his head. 'You don't believe in God,' he says. 'Remember?'

'I remember.'

'Couldn't you pretend?'

Noël sucks his brandy through his loose false teeth. 'If dipping your head graciously at prayers and singing hymns (tuneful or otherwise) with gusto is pretending, then I've been doing that for years.'

'When you die, Mr Coward, He just might surprise you.'

'Now wouldn't that be wonderful.' Noël smiles. 'Do you think He'd let me in?'

'Ask to speak to the Reverend Samson.'

'Who?'

Patrice hold up his glass, he dips a finger into it and swishes it around. 'Reverend Samson baptised me, and my brothers and sisters. He was your biggest fan, Mr Coward. He especially liked that Mad Dogs song. He would sing it at the supper club, where he'd perform several encores whether called upon or not. Reverend Samson might put in a good word, seeing as he was a man of the cloth when he was living, with a stiff white collar and all. God in His heaven might listen.'

'Reverend Samson. I'll remember to give him my calling card when I'm on the wrong side of the gates. Was he a good man?'

Patrice pulls a face. 'Well . . .' he stutters. 'Yes and no. He was very fond of a drop of rum. He liked the pretty ladies. He was a gambling man and lost most of his possessions to the poker table.'

'Are you quite sure I should mention him?'

'If you are on your way to hell, Boss, you might as well try anything.'

'I don't believe in hell.'

Patrice laughs. 'I've heard it's like Kingston on a bad Friday night.'

'Sounds perfect.'

Patrice screws up his lips. 'I'm sick to death of Kingston, I'm sick to death of Jamaica.'

'So you keep saying, but you'll miss it, you know.'

'Like you miss England, Mr Coward?'

There's a sound in Noël's head, a sound that feels like the wind whipping through the plane trees, or something pulling him down. He's in the centre of the zoetrope he had played with as a boy. Like Alice in the rabbit hole. A blurred diorama of a damp Regent's Park.

For a moment Patrice doesn't stir. He pours more brandy. He flicks away a few flying bugs with his hand. Some of the candles are sizzling and their wicks are starting to smoke.

'I will miss my brothers and sisters,' says Patrice. 'I will especially miss Theo, the youngest.'

Noël tries to stop the whirling. He puts his glass on the table. Closes his eyes. The lids fill with tears but he presses the heel of his hand against them: a temporary dam.

'I had a brother,' says Noël, quickly wiping his face with his sleeve. 'I had two. There was a baby before I was born. Russell. Meningitis took him at six. I was born later, Mother's consolation. I had a younger brother, Eric. He died a long time ago. Far too young. It was cancer.'

'I'm sorry, Boss. Were you close?'

Noël sees his brother standing on the other side of the swimming pool. He has his hands in his pockets. His head pulled down. 'We couldn't have been further apart,' he says. 'Only at the end and too late did I realise how hard it must have been for him. Mother and I were like a double act. Like Siamese twins at times. And then there was my fame and the money that went with it. Of course I worked bloody hard for it all, but Eric was more like my father – no real ambition. He was a quiet, ordinary soul. I didn't understand him.'

Patrice nods. He waits a couple of beats. 'What was it like, Boss?' he says. '"Very flat, Norfolk."'

Noël starts. 'You know *Private Lives*?'

'Not really. I started reading it last night. I'm trying to change, Boss. I am going to England. I am going to be a man of culture.'

'In Ma Henry's. In Brixton.'

'In London. I will be in London.'

'You'll have to keep reminding yourself of that, Patrice. You can't see the palace from Brixton.'

206

Patrice inhales. 'When I get myself settled,' he says slowly, 'I am going to buy a tub of Brylcreem. I am going to buy a red carnation from a girl in Covent Garden and I am going to present myself to the Ritz hotel, 150 Piccadilly, offering my services. How do I sound?'

'Pissed. Pissed as a fart.'

'We're both pissed, Boss. But my voice. Do I still sound Jamaican? I've been practising my English. I'd like to sound more Beatle than Wailer.'

'Jesus fucking Christ.'

'Father's car is a Jaguar, and Pa drives rather fast, castles, farms and draughty barns, we go charging past.'

'God.'

'For a non-believer, Mr Coward, you do call out His name a lot.'

'Just because you are going to England, you don't have to sound like Little Lord Fauntleroy.'

'I want to stand out. I want to be noticed. There are plenty of Jamaicans in London. They say the post offices are full of them.'

'Them? You.'

'Me? I'll be in Ma Henry's. She is famous for her chicken.'

'Silver service?'

'I could ask.'

'French?' says Noël.

'Probably not.'

Noël groans dramatically. 'Why have we had so much fucking brandy?' he says. 'I'll never get to my feet. My ankles won't take it. I'll collapse in a heap.'

'No, no, no.' Patrice shakes his head. 'I won't let that happen, Boss. Miguel would kill me.'

'You're as pissed as I am.'

'But I'm younger. I can take it!' Patrice leaps to his feet to demonstrate. 'See, Boss. I'm upright. I can move!' He sways towards the house. 'We need some music.'

Noël squirms. 'That's the last thing we need. And I've no fucking radio!'

'You have records!' shouts Patrice. 'Hundreds and hundreds of records!'

Noël can hardly speak. He lets his head rest in between his hands. What happened to the peace? The perfect view and the fireflies. Everything is tilting.

'Be careful!' he manages to shout. 'No scratches! No fingerprints! No dust on the needle!'

'Relax! I'm always careful, Boss,' says Patrice. 'When it comes to the music I'm a true tune vigilante.'

Noël can hear Patrice moving around the house. He hears him plugging the record player into the wall. He hears him saying 'ouch'. Suddenly a small voice drifts through the open doors. At first there is no music, just the voice. The song is familiar but it catches him off guard all the same. *'Birds flyin' high, you know how I feel, Sun in the sky, you know how I feel . . .'* Then the music widens. It fills up the space all around him. The voice expands. Nina Simone, 'Feeling Good'. Patrice moves down the steps as if he's Patrice Clarke – Live at Caesar's Palace.

When Patrice reaches the bottom of the steps – the remaining candles now looking remarkably like spotlights – he lies at Noël's feet next to the swimming pool, cigarette between his fingers, looking at the sky as Nina sings her soulful song.

Noël's eyes drop. They move across Patrice. His elegant profile. His long fingers tapping over his plain white shirt. His legs. The way his feet have made a V-shape, splaying out from his ankles. Noël's throat feels tight. He looks at his brandy glass. Resists.

The music stops. Noël can hear dust on the needle. He winces. Patrice has his eyes closed.

'You like Miss Simone?' says Noël, amazed he's remembered her name.

'She looks like my Aunt Fleur.'

'She's supposed to be difficult.'

'A diva, Boss?'

'Yes. No . . . I don't know.'

'With a voice like that, Mr Coward, she has every right to be a diva.'

'You think so?'

Patrice shrugs.

'I've met more divas than you've had hot dinners. They're a pain in the backside. I avoid them.'

Patrice rolls over, leaning on his elbow. 'And what about you, Boss? Sir Noël Diva Coward . . .'

'I'll pretend I didn't hear that.'

'I've heard you stamping your feet.'

Noël smiles despite himself. 'Only because the damn fools won't listen.'

'I listen, Boss.'

'Do you?' Noël watches Patrice's chest moving up and down. The small dark petals of skin straining at his buttonholes. He looks towards the horizon. The weeping blanket of stars.

'This time tomorrow I'll be sailing towards Rotterdam, then on to London, Boss.'

'Packing fruit.'

'It can't be that hard.'

'No.'

Most of the candles are dying. Noël wonders if he'll ever be able to stand, to leave his chair. He's grateful he doesn't need the bathroom.

'Is your world spinning, Boss?' says Patrice, getting slowly to his feet.

'Like a carousel.'

'Crazy. We need to sober up.'

Patrice walks to the other side of the swimming

pool. He sits on the edge of the concrete and lets his legs hang into the water. He slips inside. Immerses himself. He lies flat on his back, paddling his hands.

Noël sits with his cigarette. The pool and Patrice appear like a film. In the moonlight, the few fading candles, and the light from the house, the swimming pool is radiant: framed. Patrice, in his white, wet clothes looks luminous and transparent. After ten minutes he pulls himself out, his clothes clinging, his wet face shining like a seal.

'Let me help you up, Boss.' Patrice holds out his hand.

'You're not going to throw me into the swimming pool?'

'No, Boss.'

Noël has no real choice but to take his wet hand. He can feel himself slipping. He does his best to heave himself upwards and not to pull Patrice down. Their fingers entwine for safety.

'Slowly, Boss, slowly,' says Patrice.

Inside, he feels like he's on the deck of a boat in a wild crashing storm. He can hear Patrice's feet slapping on the floor tiles. A humming. They move towards the bedroom and when Noël sinks into the mattress, Patrice goes to find a towel, to dry himself off.

'You'd like your pyjamas, Boss?' says Patrice, rubbing at his hair.

'No, thank you. No pyjamas. You can leave me now.'

Noël suddenly feels sober. He manages to pull off his espadrilles. To push himself under the flimsy top cover.

'Do you need anything, Boss? Water? Your glasses? Anything at all?'

'No, Patrice. Just let me go to sleep.'

'Yes, Boss.'

Noël puts out his hand to switch off the lamp. Patrice is standing in a puddle. The towel hanging over his arm.

'Are you still here?' says Noël.

Patrice nods. 'I am going to London tomorrow. The boat sails at seven-thirty. From Kingston.'

'Well, goodbye, Patrice. Good luck. Give my regards to the Ritz.'

'I'll do that, Mr Coward.'

Noël turns off the lamp. For a few long seconds Patrice doesn't move. When he closes his eyes Noël can hear him padding downstairs. The click of the door. The key as it turns inside the lock. Hours later, when he wakes to use the bathroom, he sees a pattern of footprints. The damp towel on the rail. He holds it to his face. It smells of salt and detergent. He sleeps with it coiled tightly round his hand. It feels like the rain.

IN THE early hours of Monday 26 March 1973, after years of ill health, Noël Coward had a heart attack and died.

He was at Firefly.

Miguel found him. At his side was a half-read copy of *The Enchanted Castle* by E. Nesbit.

# ACKNOWLEDGEMENTS

THANKS TO Poppy Hampson, Silvia Crompton and all the team at Chatto. My agent, David Miller. To my friend and fellow writer John Boyne, who was so enthusiastic about this novel from the start. The Sumner family. To my family, Simon, Emily, Mum, Kevan, Ruth, Joanne, Karen and all their clan.